THE
SNOW
COLLECTORS

A NOVEL

TINA MAY HALL

DZANC
BOOKS

5220 Dexter Ann Arbor Rd.
Ann Arbor, MI 48103
www.dzancbooks.org

This is a work of fiction. Names, characters, businesses, places, events, locales, and incidents are either the products of the author's imagination or used in a fictitious manner. Sir John and Lady Jane Franklin are real-life historical figures and many of the details included here are true, but many are made up for the sheer pleasure of it.

First US edition: February 2020
Interior design by Michelle Dotter
ISBN: 9781950539048

Printed in the United States of America

10   9   8   7   6   5   4   3   2   1

For Tycho, who was born in a snowstorm

CHAPTER ONE

I FOUND THE DEAD WOMAN at the edge of my woods on the last day of January. King month. Thirty-one spikes on a crown of icicles. I had moved to a place where it snowed nearly all year round, and when it wasn't snowing, the landscape exploded into damp and flower. The afternoon was warm, all of thirteen degrees in the shelter of the trees. When the clouds blew apart, I stopped snowshoeing to lift my face to the sky. I had lived here only seven months, and I was still hungry for light. The locals assured me that would pass.

A year before I moved, my parents and twin sister had disappeared in a boating accident, lost at sea, their yacht never found, their bodies gone forever into the salt and dark. I liked to think of them as seals, sleek as wishes, slipping away. Once, when Claire and I were seven or eight, a fisherman had traded my father a sealskin for a painting. We had to sneak into his studio to touch it. The skin was silk if you stroked it one way, sandpaper the other. We buried our faces in it and took turns wearing it as a cape. It smelled like a potato, freshly dug. We had dreams of swimming after wearing it. Our throats hurt in the mornings after those dreams, as if we had been singing all night.

❄

Every schoolchild knows water holds memories better than any other substance. We've transcribed the chemical equations that prove this, and we learned early on that there is no remedy for it. In the year after their boat disappeared, I saw my parents and sister many times walking on the beach, ducking behind the black boulders at the north end, bending over the tide pools to wring out their sodden hair. I never could walk quickly enough to catch them, though I ran barefoot on the sand, at all hours, in all weather. So I left my seaside home, with its gritty old carpet and flapping windows and conch shell–bordered garden of weeds and grasses, and drove east in my father's green Plymouth to start anew. He and my mother had both been artists, one of those couples so in love with each other you fear for their children, but I'd had Claire and she'd had me, and when we all went out as a family, it was as if we were on a double date. Claire and I had even had a secret language, in the way of twins. Ours was a kind of sign language that had evolved to icons, hieroglyphs that showed up in Claire's art. She had followed in our parents' footsteps, taken the best of our sculptor mother and our painter father and parlayed it into a talent for faces. She did portraits of artists—ancient, contemporary, and everything in between. Some of her paintings took up a whole wall, like the image of Titian reclining, nude and ascetic, beaked and bearded, on the side of the recycling depot. Some of them were the size of a pocket watch. She painted three hundred seventy-eight pictures of our parents, always together, always touching, before she vanished. For all I know, she was painting another, laughingly posing them cheek to cheek, when their boat slipped over the edge of the world.

❋

One day, while snowshoeing after a winter storm, I found a body at the edge of my woods. The first thing I saw was her hand under the low-hanging hawthorn branches. Her hand, covered in snow, making the sign Claire and I devised for sun—a cup, an ark, a shape to catch the light.

❄

I was the only member of my family not an artist. They stretched behind me in long lines of knotted hair and paint-stained lips, of lead poisoning and chipped nails, of tables piled with decaying pears and pineapples and lilies browning on the stem. I wrote entries for an encyclopedia. I used a manual typewriter for the first drafts. I liked the small blows of the keys. My specialty was water.

❄

The day I snowshoed into my woods and found a body, I was contemplating my riches. The sun sifted through the firs. The snow broke under my feet. Three life insurance policies had made me a fairly wealthy woman. I did not need to write encyclopedia entries and live in the snow. I liked the small blows. I liked writing about water, turning its dark and froth into bitter-smelling ink, blocked paragraphs to be folded and stamped and sent away.

I had an orange from California in my pocket. The snow was a skin to be broken. My lungs hurt with each breath. My twin's dog ran ahead of me. I was orphaned, too old for an evil stepmother, my bequest a barn full of art and a basset hound named Rembrandt.

❄

After my family disappeared, I grew quiet and cold. Every day made me harder. It was a wonderful feeling. No one to give account to, all those fringes folding in. There was a recklessness in grief. I didn't care about anyone but myself and didn't want for anything. I was a being without desire.

✳

In the first clearing, I peeled the orange, its oily skin staining my hands. I threw the rind in the snow, and Rembrandt sniffed at it disdainfully. It was my land; I could do what I pleased. I was no longer someone anyone would want as a friend. The plump sections burst against my teeth.

✳

Our parents named us Henna and Claire. I was dark; she was light. We had the same crooked canine tooth. I was born four minutes before her, and I cried for sixteen months without stopping. My mother hid me in the laundry basket, under loosely piled towels, when she couldn't stand it any longer. Claire was born with long hair, a sign of patience. She was a chubby baby even though I stole her food. My parents spent one weekend wrapping her in plaster, her folds of flesh were so dear to them.

Ahead of me was another clearing and another and another. Rembrandt loved them all. He darted ahead, baying and rolling, and sometimes fled into the trees not to be seen for ten or fifteen minutes. Undoubtedly he was tracking things, eating deer poop and gnawing on old bones, digging up god knows what. He liked to be a wolf in the woods, slinking behind snowdrifts and trees. His periodic leaping out at me was the dog equivalent of a joke.

✳

Water was my specialty. Few people studied hydrology because it required a particular combination of intuition and mathematical skill. I had spent years mapping molecules, perfecting the extraction of sorrow and love, magnesium and lead, making water potable again in a world that had exhausted its tributaries. Corporations and townships would have paid me a lot to approve certain practices. They had in the past. It used to be that water rose at my touch, but after my family disappeared, after I'd hardened, water no longer answered me. Instead, I chose to write encyclopedia entries about the Arctic and those who had trespassed upon its ice and snow. My editor at the encyclopedia thought I was eccentric because I always sent her a hard copy. I typed in black ink on blue paper, scented with violets, sealed with indigo wax.

❄

One day, while snowshoeing after a winter storm, I found a body at the edge of my woods. I saw the cup of her hand first, half submerged in the snow. Rembrandt nudged it and I called to him, held him by the collar and dragged him with me as I searched for a stick to push the spiky branches aside. The police would later make much of this, my willingness to delay the uncovering. The dead woman was curled under the low-hanging branches of a hawthorn bush, facing me. She was wearing a thin pink T-shirt and jeans, and I shivered to see her. The red of her lips was striking. *Wine? Lipstick?* Everything went hot, then cold, and my stomach lurched. Her eyes were closed, as if she were asleep under a film of frost, waiting for a kiss.

❄

A sound overhead startled me, and I let the stick drop; I heard it hit flesh. In the tree beside me, five crows complained loudly. For the first time, I thought the word *murder*. I looked around me to see how the landscape had changed. I could see nothing out of place, just the thick sky and the bare trees and my tracks in the snow, shadows gouged into the white.

❄

The police chief stood in my kitchen, nursing his tea. His brown hair was shot through with gold, and he looked more like a surfer than law enforcement. As a teenager, I was partial to the surfer boys, their muscles and their grace, their lidded stares and their careless drawls. Best of all was the ease with which they contemplated my paste-up home with its marble dust and smells of turpentine, the nude fat ladies flat on the walls and the molding fruit piled on silver platters. Those surfer boys just wanted a stolen beer from the refrigerator and some sweet grappling on the porch swing. So straightforward, so easily distracted. Claire and I ourselves surfed evenings, when the water turned platinum and rose, and the salt dried in goosebumps on our upper arms. We ran down from our house to the setting sun, into the scent of tar and urine, wearing the memory of seal.

❄

Snow melted into the cuffs of the police chief's grey polyester pants. His men left muddy footprints on the hardwood floor of my kitchen. "Dogs have been at her," he said, as if it was a test, and Rembrandt snorted from his position by the door. Inside the house, the dog was imperturbable, lazy, obese, and old, obsessed with his genitalia and whatever might fall from the counter. One young officer whose ears were bright red from the cold couldn't stop describing the body, despite the chief's stern look. No signs of violence besides the animals, he reported excitedly. "She could be your sister," he said.

"I don't have a sister," I replied, and the chief seemed disappointed, as if for a moment he had believed the mystery could be solved so easily. I didn't even feel a twinge. My heart was down deep, at the bottom of the sea, where only blind and armored things survived. It was dark by then, and I studied my reflection in the window over the sink, wondering if I looked like a dead woman. A radio hissed, calling the chief and his officers back into the woods.

❄

Sometimes, I liked to think my family was on some kind of extended voyage, an adventure in the high seas, an expedition to map unknown waters. Most of the time, I knew what had really happened. I knew they were sinking ever deeper. But sometimes I imagined them reading my wax-dotted letters, my violet-tinged epistles. I liked to think they were writing back, leaving me messages in places I hadn't yet discovered.

❄

Directly after they'd disappeared, I spent a good chunk of my savings hiring crews to go out looking for them. We collected a lot of trash masquerading as clues—somebody's friendship bracelet twined with algae, a plastic poncho, infinite numbers of partnerless flip-flops and galoshes, scuffed canteens to test for DNA. And eventually the guys at the dock got bored, tired of my tears, my pleas, my insistence on staying out into the dusk, my claims that my family were the sturdy sort who might survive at sea for days, even weeks. When I was down to the last boat that would take my money, a beat-up trawler leaking oil and splinters, I traded the sour old captain ribald jokes and a perfunctory blow job in exchange for staying out all night, raking the waves with a guttering search light. And I didn't regret it one bit—in fact, welcomed the salt on my tongue, felt close to Claire then, taste of seawater. The men did some illegal fishing while I swept the light back and forth. The fish were flurries of metal shards in the nets, and the skin around my eyes swelled in the spray until the world narrowed to a slit, dark unto dark, the sounds of mermaids coughing, the clatter of bodies falling onto deck.

❄

I stayed at the kitchen window, watching myself drinking tea, feeling the cold seeping in around the edges. When they brought her out of the woods, they carried her on a stretcher, shrouded, bound with heavy straps. Their flashlights brightened and dimmed like torches or candles—some strange procession for a queen, a saint, and I the only spectator.

❄

I'm telling you, there was liberation in misanthropy. I used to be the life of the party. I used to be a golden-skinned girl, with Claire beside me in skirts we'd made ourselves, with signature drinks and laughs and plastic rings in the shape of flowers. Now, I was the strange dark-haired woman in the coffee shop, the grocery store, the village library. Yes, I lived in a village, or so the green road sign declared. That was part of the reason I moved there. I liked the idea of a place that still had villages and grist stones and cider mills and sprawling Victorian mansions with black shutters and attics and topiary gardens. All so removed from the ocean, with its loose undulations and hammered-together shacks.

I tried to fit in. I wore high-necked blouses and severely tailored blazers. I owned many pairs of knee socks and boots with multiple hooks for the laces. I longed for a corset. The villagers seemed to wear exclusively sweaters from Vermont or Ireland or Peru. I'd never seen such a wooly bunch.

❄

It was difficult to sleep that night, even with Rembrandt sprawled wheezing against me. I'd locked all the windows and doors without any clear idea of what I feared. A dead woman couldn't hurt me. At dawn, the bells from the tall-steepled church rang in town. Their echoes floated up the hill to my house, joined the tapping of frozen branches at my window, persistent ghosts, demanding entry.

CRYOSPHERE

*T*HE SNOW COLLECTORS HAD RECORDS going back to medieval times. There was a shelf in the Bodleian dedicated to them. Times, temperatures, durations. But the real collection was scattered in attics and studies, buried in molding trunks and locked away in desk drawers for which the keys had long since disappeared. All over the world, small bottles rattled in the dark—meticulously labeled vials, washed and stripped tonic jars, flasks stoppered with clay and wax. The snow samples bore the dates of their falling and the coordinates of their occasion. Snow collectors had their unique methodologies—some gathered only from the same month each year, some concentrated on variations within a single county or city, and some collected according to latitude, amassing rows of vials organized from south to north or vice versa. These last were the most obsessive, often paying great sums for snow from the farthest reaches, or trading favors that stretched on through generations. The most driven were those who actually traveled to the Arctic and Antarctic, always under false pretenses, since snow collecting was frowned upon and viewed as a particularly ugly perversion.

Beyond the times and dates and degrees, the true snow collector had evolved to keeping a more surprising record. Each sample was to be etched with an emotion, an intuitive assignment. In the hands of some collectors, this was a simple as one word affixed to the vial—*love* or *envy* or *contentment*. For others it was a calling card's worth of impressions—*the brush of the snow like a mother's fingertips on one's cheek at night, the smell of woodsmoke and lye, the sound of carts clattering in the street.* For the collectors at the center of the movement, the ones who met secretly at country house parties and London bookshops, the ones who built vaults to their preoccupation in the walls of their houses, the ones for whom a snowstorm was a mixture of arousal and shame, for these collectors, the records were bulky as novels, in some cases *were* novels, published without readers knowing the narrative was a comprehensive unraveling of the space of a snowfall, the passions and losses of a particular storm. Always, there was the physical referent of the snow sample, sloshing in the glass, that ever-bitter reminder of the ephemerality of their obsession.

CHAPTER TWO

OUR PARENTS MADE OUR GIFTS when we were children, no matter how we begged for plastic dolls and butane-powered roller skates. One year they gave us each a small egg, pale blue wrapped in gold foil. We slept with the eggs balanced in the hollows of our throats to keep them warm. After three weeks, the shells cracked and tiny clockwork birds hopped out, mine green, Claire's red. I fed mine worms until it stopped working, but Claire kept hers in a matchbox lined with dried seaweed and it sang us to sleep every night for a year.

❋

The next morning, snow fell in spurts before descending in a steady curtain. I went back to the spot where I found the woman, wanting to see it again before it was covered over. The police tracks crisscrossed mine. The teeth of my snowshoes ripped at the yellow tape. Rembrandt dug his nose into the snow and tossed arcs of it into the air. Then he ran off into the woods, crazed by the everlasting winter. Dusk settled in. I should have brought a flashlight, or better yet, a lantern. Fire was more certain in the North.

The space around the hawthorn bush was excavated, scraped down to bare dirt frosted with new snow. On my hands and knees, I crawled under the boughs, into that dark place where the snow had drifted. Thorns tore at me as I circled like an animal looking for a spot to lie down. The temptation was to arrange myself in her position, to see what she might have seen. I burrowed deeper into the bush and felt something with my fingertips, something round and smooth. As my hand closed over it, I heard footsteps deeper in the forest, approaching. I tried to turn back, to get to my feet, but thorns and branches trapped me, sank into my hair and the fleece of my jacket. I jerked at the twigs, panicked, but stopped, entangled, immobile, as the deliberate crunching of the snow grew louder. Someone was standing on the other side of the hawthorn; a darker shadow was visible through its dense branches. I couldn't tell if I had been seen. I stayed silent, caught in a bad murder mystery, listening for someone else's breath, hearing only the sound of my own pulse.

In graduate school, they had taught us that blood is very similar to water except that it resists traveling long distances. We did experiments in which we pricked our thumbs with silver lancets and let the drops fall onto a slide, then moved the slide to a lab table a few feet away. Invariably, though almost imperceptibly, the blood would move toward the edge of the slide closest to our hearts. If we walked to the other side of the room, the blood followed us, like a flower tracking the sun. But the dead woman had not bled, and I was wearing gloves; there was no reason for my hands to be wet.

I plunged them into the snow, keeping hold of the small object I'd found, reaching for the water I knew was locked in the earth. Nothing. A year and a half without being able to feel water's hum. I dug deeper, until my flesh was burning with cold, and I felt a tiny vibration run through the hard thing in my hand, a whisper of some sort, discordant against my skin, but still enough to make my heart clutch. The footsteps had been silent for some time now and I could no longer see a shadow—either the person had left or was waiting for me to stop scrabbling uselessly under the shrubbery. I yanked myself free of the branches and stumbled backward, into the clearing. There was nothing, no one waiting, just the dark woods, the trees turning black in the twilight, the snow still falling, each flake winking out the day, no sounds of fleeing.

In my palm was a smooth black pebble with a white vein, small as an almond, polished and clean. The kind of stone you'd find on a beach, tossed up like a gift by the tide.

❄

Mornings, I typed in the office I'd made of the sun porch. It was cold in there, especially as I had to keep the doors to the house closed so that Rembrandt didn't pillage the kitchen while I was working. He lay by one of the doors and licked and licked and licked. I reminded myself I liked the small blows. Arctic explorers were so sincere with their maps and charcoals and logbooks. One man's job was to melt snow for water all day long. Sometimes I felt like an old woman, safe in my brittle bones. Sometimes a young girl flickered in me, Claire dancing, clutching at my tender throat.

When things became unbearable, I'd go to the library.

❄

The village library had a tower and a substantial collection of Arctic literature and materials. Folios of expedition drawings and a first edition of Elisha Kent Kane's diaries were one long winding staircase removed from paperback tales of serial killers and hauntings and thwarted love that bloomed in final pages. This was a great boon for me. I spent hours in the funny round room with its wheeled ladders and narrow windows. The day heated and ice slid down the building in sheets. My editor was accommodating, sent all things North my way. There was an uptick in interest in polar terminology now that the ice mass was nearly extinct.

Locked in the stone tower, the frostbitten explorers roamed unending plains of white. And I plucked them from those bleak expanses, sucked a little of their marrow and sent it on in blackened capsules.

✾

The librarian was a wizened man named Harris who also served beer at the tavern. He was very pleasant as he proffered the key to the collection, a skeleton key of course, tarnished and rough. Harris had a disproportionately large moustache that was yellowed at its swooping tips and blazed palely against his dark skin. His hair needed trimming and his plaid shirts all looked the same. He was one of four non-white people in the village, as far as I knew. I'd never seen him in a sweater. When he stamped the mysteries I loved to borrow, he did so in green ink, a date that smeared, and briskly stacked the volumes flush, wincing a little when I tumbled them into the vintage doctor's bag I used instead of a satchel. The bag was black leather, cracking in places, and smelled of linseed oil. I'd found it in an antique store north of town. It seemed like something my father would have used to lug his paints around, and so I'd bought it, a false memory, the safest kind.

There was only the one key, and Harris was compulsive about it, so I had to trek up the stairs to unlock the tower door and then back down to hang the key on its assigned hook. Villagers were scarce in the library, except on Tuesdays, during story hour, when windblown young mothers and their roly-poly toddlers sprawled on the rug in the children's section. Harris read in a Western twang and never bothered to hold the book out so the kids could see the pictures, but they were transfixed nonetheless, clapping and giggling in the right places, watching him as if expecting him to pull doves from his pockets while their mothers dozed, upright, through three or four happy endings. On the other days, Harris would invite me to share his tea after I'd been working a few hours, Lipton on the hot plate and vanilla wafers. "Henna," he'd say, "You're covered in dust," and shake his head, amused at the way some people make their livings.

❉

Afternoons, I prepared my missives and walked Rembrandt. I bleached the sink and washed solitary dishes. I swept the sandy gravel used on roadways from the wood floors. I waxed and shone and polished. Every window gleamed; the sheets were redolent of fabric softener and hot iron. Need it be said that I was tired? When I slept, I dreamt Claire and Claire again. I dreamt the months of waiting by the ocean, watching for flotsam, imagining bodies in burrows of seaweed and fishing line. How odd it was that a body had washed up finally, a sister-girl whom no one claimed, and yet I didn't dream the dead woman, just Claire pulling at me like a needle drawing the thread behind it.

❉

I bought stamps at the post office. It was a small white building, quaint and federal. The stamps were Mary Cassatt scenes, tiny portraits, girls at the seashore, sun hats and pinafores, a self-adhesive mosaic of blues and wheaty yellows. The postmistress had red hair and a formidable bust. "Hear you had some excitement at your place," she said, her index finger anchoring the sheet of stamps to the wood-grained counter. In another life, she would have been my bullish aunt. In another life, we would have been sipping sherry and staring at the moors.

The post office parking lot was all ice, slick and cloudy over the asphalt. The police chief pulled into the space next to mine. Black pickup, unnaturally clean for winter. I thought *turtle wax* and *chamois*. He jumped out, lithe and smiling. "You should stop by the station sometime," he called as I opened the door of my car. The ice beneath my feet splintered. An invitation, an order.

❉

Three old men sat outside the bakery/coffee shop no matter the weather. A few weeks ago, I'd seen them on their cast-iron bench in a blizzard. They wore newsboy caps, all three, in plaid and tweed and black wool. They spoke in a brogue, from lack of teeth, I supposed. "Fine day," they always cast at me as I went in to buy my bagels. "Good boy-o you are," they slurred at Rembrandt who waited outside, slouched beside them, compulsively licking the bakery window until he saw his sourdough bun placed in the bag. Then he'd flop to the ground and investigate his back haunch, content. The old men were too well-bred for weather. Nothing could surprise them, even a newcomer like myself. The first day I'd come down the hill to town, the old men greeted me, recited my address, and pursed doughy mouths. Since then, I'd tended to ignore them, those three fates, with their newspapers and their paper cups of coffee and the stoic slump of their shoulders. No doubt about it, they knew what was coming, and I wanted nothing to do with them.

❋

I waited a day to go to the police station, feeling coy. It was another white building, this one tall and skinny, wedged between the limestone bank and the yellow-sided bed and breakfast. In the village square, the children threw snowballs. The baker carried old bread to the trash bin. The parson stuck plastic letters spelling *blessing* on the black felt board next to the church door. The tiny decaying movie theater's lights blinked on. *Die Hard* had been playing the entire time I'd lived there, and there was always a line outside on Friday nights. It was afternoon and the toes of my boots pinched. But they were so wonderfully witchy, pointed snakeskin, sharp as railroad spikes.

The police chief's office was a small wood-paneled room. The dispatcher mixed us Ovaltine, her cat-eye glasses sparkling. "Call me Fletcher," the police chief said, and showed a bit of tooth. He placed his hand over mine on the desk at one point, and I felt a jolt as electric as in any romance novel. Everything about him was heat, from the gold in his hair to the mirth in his eyes to the warmth radiating from his skin to mine. He asked if there was anything else I could remember, why I had taken my time getting back to the house. He asked whether I carried a cell phone in the woods and had I heard anything and when did I sleep and wake and where. I said I couldn't help him. Nothing had occurred to me; I was as puzzled as he.

❄

I lied, of course, and my boots were stained by the sidewalk salt. A white mark dried over the instep. I had taken something from the dead woman, from that outstretched hand. It was a scrap of paper, the edge of a letter, black-bordered, the lower left corner. What else could it be but a clue? The fragment read *Bedford* and under that, *Wednesday* and then at the very right edge of the paper, the start of a signature, one name, *Jane*, the J firm as iron, no open loops, just one stricken line.

POLE STARS

*J*ANE GREW UP MOTHERLESS. WHEN she was lonely, she read *The Mysteries of Udolpho* and dreamt of carriage rides along a stormy precipice. She made lists. She kept an obsessive daily record, her journal-books, crabbed hand, lines written on both sides, which she revised, blacked out, burned, excised. There were holes in all of her pages. In Van Diemen's Land, she paid a shilling bounty for each dead snake, until they numbered twelve thousand; some were sent to her in the post, rotting. She never knew about the snow collectors, but she kept her own box of famous waters from her travels, stored in blue-tinged vials, siphoned up by her own hand. Everywhere she went, people gave her things—a feathered royal cloak in Hawaii, silk slippers in Algiers, an enameled beetle in Odessa, a tin stove in Sitka. She helped stock the 1867 Paris Exposition. Her drawing room was the envy of all. Her lists grew longer and longer. She wrote in blue notebooks, small enough to carry with her. She stitched their leaves herself.

When she was young and imagining love, she always pictured a dinner party, she and her husband, weights on a scale, balancing the table, every glass and plate gleaming. She pictured swimming in a warm river, the feeling of water holding her up, the current moving through her. She wrote about these things in her notebooks and then cut them out and tossed them into the fireplace like so many fingernail parings, little bits of herself flaring up. She imagined her husband touching the skin on the inside of her elbow, kissing her throat, then higher, and lower. She imagined her husband graceful as a barque in the stream, strong enough to carry her wherever she desired.

CHAPTER THREE

*W*HY DID I LIE TO the police chief? Maybe I thought it was negligible, something that could be of no possible use. The handwriting seemed to belong to another century; the paper was brittle. This was no proof of an assignation. Maybe I thought I could do a better job investigating than the police. I had, as yet, seen no evidence of perspicacity. Maybe I thought it was a message for me, grown out of the snow, carried a continent by clouds and wind.

I came home to find Rembrandt had gotten into the pantry. The string I'd used to fasten the knob to a hook on the doorframe was broken. He had scattered a package of alphabet pasta across the kitchen and the living room and was perched on the sofa, chewing the box. The pasta had been left by the house's previous owners, so I swept it up with no remorse, not surprised by the lack of any intelligible words.

Rembrandt seemed happy with the cardboard so I left him there, dripping pulpy gobs onto the nubby linen—"Flaxseed," the salesman had said when I'd bought it. "One of our most popular neutrals."

✻

Over the olive bar at the supermarket in the nearest town, one of my neighbors asked me to dinner. "Short notice, I know," she said gaily, as if this made the invitation more enticing. She was a tall woman with beige fondant hair and matching leather tote with big gold buckles. "Bring a bottle of something yummy," she said as she sailed off, steering her cart with brute force through the throng around the deli counter. I was shocked into compliance, kalamatas rolling from my limp spoon. The roasted red peppers had the springiness of something flayed.

✳

Everyone else had cloaked their wine in skinny flowered and striped paper bags with yarn handles. They averted their eyes from my naked bottle. It seemed I had become some kind of celebrity. "What was it like?" our hostess asked, holding out a tray of puff pastry filled with creamed mushrooms. The host was genial enough, generous with the gin. He wore a bow tie and a cashmere vest. "It could have been any one of us," said a woman with a pearl comb holding up one side of her hair, and I couldn't work out if she meant killed or surprised by a dead woman in the woods.

The police chief came in just before we were ushered to the table with its long flaxseed runner and its bowls of roses. "Chief," I nodded.

"Call me Fletcher," he said to me, and touched my shoulder briefly. Heat bloomed. The host clanged the butter knife against his wineglass for a toast, but once we were silent, he had nothing to say.

✳

Even though I didn't smoke, I went out on the porch for an after-dinner cigarette with the police chief and the hostess's teenage stepdaughter. The snowflakes dropped like coins in the light of the streetlamps. Then the power failed and everything went dark. Shrieks rose from inside the house.

"We should have dinner sometime," the police chief said, presumably to me, since the stepdaughter had started speed-texting the second the street went black.

"I believe we just did," I said.

"You're a cold woman, Henna." He seemed pleased to say it. As I basked in the laughter in his voice, I felt a quiver, down low—lower than I would have expected for flirtation, far beneath me, a strand of water vibrating. My heart stretched to meet it, blood parched from all the months of silence. Something rolled under the toe of my boot. I bent down to touch it: a smooth stone, gray as water, bisected by a dull white band.

❋

At home, the power was still off. I typed by candlelight. Rembrandt gnawed happily on the chicken carcass he had exhumed from the trash while I was gone. I decided to let him live dangerously. The windows of the sun porch were as opaque as marble, dimly showing me my own wavering form.

One pane pinged sharply as something hit it from the outside. Maybe a bit of hail or a deer antler. An owl's claw or vampire's fang. Maybe the knife point of a murderer or the pebble of a lover. Who knew what was out there? The only certainty was that I was surrounded by glass and feeble light, and anyone who wished could watch me sitting upright at my desk, unperturbed, fingers steady.

❋

"Natural causes, exposure and the cold," the police chief said when he called to tell me how the woman had died. This was a courtesy he proffered because she was found on my land, I supposed, and thus a tiny bit my property. Rembrandt hated the phone ringing;

he considered it a peculiar indignity that required much barking in response. "We're still trying to figure out to whom she belongs," the police chief said as if he read my mind. I thought of the hard frozen ground, thought of my old explorers who had to cache their dead in the winter, well away from the sled dogs and anywhere wild animals could get at them. "How about that dinner?" he said, and I had to admire his timing.

After I hung up, I felt guilty. Something in his voice made me feel found out, as if he knew I was holding something back, so I took the stolen clue from the book where I'd hidden it. A rusty blue-backed copy of *Rebecca* that had come with the house. The scrap of paper glared, the white of a clenched knuckle or a furrowed brow. Its black border was ominous, sour-smelling, but I tucked it into the pocket of my coat anyway, so as to have it with me the next time I went into town.

❄

Later that night, the glass of the sun porch pinged again, and I put aside my notes on scientific instruments used on polar voyages to go investigate. The snow shone mutely. No one was there. My land stretched out before me, hiding who knew what. I was not inclined to tramp through it looking for more bodies. I thought again of the police chief, the laughter like molasses in his voice, his broad shoulders and the smell of starch and metal he carried with him. Again, that quivering. I followed it as if it were a thread, and it led me around the side of the house, to the glass wall of the sun porch.

In the shadows at its base, something waited. I plucked it from the snow—another pebble, gray and white. I was calling stones instead of water, a beginner's mistake. But it was the first sign I'd had of my talent since Claire died. My throat clenched, as if the stone were lodged there, and I cried as I hadn't since the news of their boat's disappearance. The moon tore cloud after cloud from its face. Every-thing stung, prickling like a limb awakening.

❄

I read grim stories in the big city newspaper. I wished my family had been killed in their beds while they slept, or burned to death in a nightclub, or murdered by religious extremists on video in the desert. I wished I had their bodies to wash. I wished I had a trio of graves, that their bones were safe underground.

❄

One night at 2 a.m., I sat up thinking, *Jane*, and remembered blue skin, toenails black with cold. Why would the woman have been barefoot in winter? Why without a coat? She could not have come far. A couple of miles at the most, I'd guess. She was none of my concern, and yet she was a particularly persistent guest. "No signs of violence," the red-eared officer had said. If not murder, what?

As teenagers, Claire and I had read all the gothic novels we could find, especially the more recent ones, filled with creepy houses and romances featuring wry heroines who had to choose between the om-inously gallant swain and the less likely cousin or brother or neigh-bor. Sometimes there were ghosts—or weirder inheritances. Bodies positively littered those tales, and none by accident; no drowning or sudden illness or disappearance was without reason. Claire thought the books hilarious and kept a tally of secret passageways. I regarded them as a means of divination, and slept with them under my pil-low, dreamt unveilings and hard edges and text like maggots writhing beneath my cheek.

❄

I crept out of bed; Rembrandt snored on, one back leg thrust straight into the air. At the top of the stairs, I hesitated. The lower level was a pool of darkness. I never thought to turn on the lights; they seemed an offense that time of night. I plunged down the stairs before I lost my nerve, reciting Petrarch silently for balance.

My coat with the scrap of letter in its pocket was in the room off the kitchen, where the boots and plastic bags of ice melt were kept. The dining room I navigated by counting chairs, but stopped at the swinging door to the kitchen. Surely that was a line of light under the door and the sounds of rummaging. I crouched behind the door, wondering if the gap at the floor was wide enough to see anything. And then I heard it. Breathing, just a handspan away from me. Someone was listening to me listening. My own breath stopped, clamped into my chest by the kick of adrenaline, and I waited. Claire and I used to have contests to see who could hold their breath longer. Her record was four and a half days, but I could always dive deeper.

There was a whisper of a sound from the kitchen, a shoe dragged clumsily across the floor. I felt dizzy, put my hand down to steady myself, and touched a slimy mass with a hard core that rolled under my palm. I fell forward just as the door swung out sharply to meet me, and everything went loud, then still.

POLAR DRIFT

*T*HEY CALLED HIM "THE MAN who ate his boots" because on one Arctic expedition he had been reduced to gnawing the deerskin to stave off the pangs. One of his crew had turned to murder to procure a more succulent feast, and Captain Franklin executed him. Even in dire circumstances, some things were not to be tolerated. For the rest of his life, he had a weakness for fat. He liked the tender bits, the globules, ate butter straight, ordered the roast be plump as a lady's cheek. He wooed Jane with a gift of reindeer tongues which she did not eat even when he assured her they were a delicacy. He named a snow-covered point for her and told her stories about a sun and moon that never set. He made it romantic for her and did not mention madness nor the stench.

His first wife had been a poet and a friend of Jane's. She hadn't liked to leave the house, but Jane had convinced her to go on long carriage rides during which they discussed Captain Franklin and kept the windows shut tight. When she died, she left Jane her gloves and a lock of hair. Jane kept these items; she had never traveled light. On the day she married Captain Franklin, Jane considered wearing the brooch of his first wife's hair, as a tribute, but instead lined her bodice with the pages from her own journals that she had torn out to burn. By the time her dress was removed later, they had combusted, flameless, ashless, hadn't left a trace.

CHAPTER FOUR

I WOKE NEXT TO A small puddle of blood—my own, I realized, as I felt the gash on my forehead where the edge of the door had caught me. Some grotesque splintered bony thing loomed in my vision. One of Rembrandt's ubiquitous rawhides, I identified at the same time I noticed the lights were on. This gave me a start, but I was on my feet immediately, undeterred by my negligible wound. The front door was open, the entryway chilly. I must have been out for a bit. I peered down the blank shoveled sidewalk, no fresh snow to reveal footprints. In the kitchen, nothing seemed out of place. My coat still hung in the mudroom. The scrap of letter was still in the pocket. One pane of the window in the mudroom door was broken. There was glass on the floor, and next to the washing machine, a large smooth rock, black striped with white.

❄

There has been an intrusion, I thought as I held the bag of frozen stir-fry vegetables to my head. The glass was swept up. The rock was placed with the others on my sunroom desk. A dead woman was making disorder of the order I'd so carefully constructed. The front door still stood open; I could feel the cold coming in.

❄

The next morning, I walked across to my neighbor's house to see if she had duct tape and cardboard for the broken pane. The day was bright and cloudless, so rare for this part of the world. The sky was enameled blue. While I waited for Mariel to answer the door, I contemplated the hedge of dormant forsythia against her house, perfectly pruned against the stone cottage. The shutters were soft green; smoke threaded from the chimney. It was the house of a good witch. I often told Mariel so.

She was my one friend in town, so far. When I moved in, she had come over with a big basket of bread and her ever-present notepad. The bread was in fat braids, and nestled between them was a small glass jar of honey. I gasped when I saw it, honey was such a rarity. Mariel kept bees in pristine hives in her part of the woods.

Today, when she opened the door, her eyes went straight to the bruise on my forehead. She ushered me in, unhurried as ever, but clearly concerned, fingers brushing over the tops of bookshelves and end tables, searching for a pen. Mariel could not speak or chose not to. In the kitchen, she pulled one out of a jar, all identical, silver pens filled with silver ink. If she had a voice, it would have sounded like bells. But she didn't reach for her notepad. Instead she turned and selected a small white ceramic pot from the top shelf over her sink.

She dipped her fingers into the pot and then smeared the salve on my forehead. It was cool and smelled of pine. Only then did she pull her notepad toward her to write *Arnica*. Mariel sat back and smiled at me, her cropped white hair neat as always, her white tunic and pants unwrinkled. She always wore white. She told me once that it calmed the bees. I found it peaceful too, and I leaned my head back onto the hard wooden chair as I told her my story.

❄

I was trying to show Mariel the sign language Claire and I had shared. It was slow going. I had no word for bee. By the time Claire and I were born, the bees had all disappeared. The ones Mariel kept were genetic resurrections of an ancient Turkish strain. They thrived in cold and damp and fed on many things other than pollen. She had told me their wings were formed of some kind of latex-coated cornstarch. Their honey was dark gold and tasted of moss and roses.

When I was done talking, Mariel made us tea. Mine was mint, hers licorice. The steam knit us together. I felt safe there, as if her tight little cottage really were enspelled. Around her neck, she wore a silver cylinder on a long chain. I had never seen her open it, but now she did, unscrewing the metal cap and tipping a bit of powder out onto her fingertip. She touched the back of my hand, leaving a dusty orange streak. I couldn't tell what it was, perhaps pollen or dried honey, maybe ground-up wings. Mariel squinted at me and tapped her thumbs together, the sign for luck.

❄

I searched the map first, based on the scant clues from the letter fragment. There was a Bedford Road just south of town. It was lined with vinyl-sided estates, naked on their reclaimed farmland, no tree in sight. The road ended at a meat processing plant. Though hunting season was surely over, two men stood by a pickup truck from the bed of which four legs poked up, raw flesh divested of its skin. The men looked at me with the slow gaze that only people in this part of the country can manage. It's a stare grown of belonging to one place four hundred years.

I circled in the parking lot, skidded a little on the packed snow, retreated back down the curving road lined with modern ameni-ties—plastic bubble skylights and synthetic marble countertops, whirlpool baths and high-quality imitation wood-grain decks. Everything so hopeful, so new, so seemingly impervious to the elements that I couldn't help but imagine it in ruins, grown over, gnawed by rodents. Water will always flow downhill, no matter what it is running to meet.

❄

Rembrandt and I stopped by the police station. I have never had any patience with heroines who blunder on alone past the point of reason. Although it was clearly too late to mention the bit of paper, the break-in must be reported. The police chief was not there, but the dispatcher admired Rembrandt and gave him rough scratches behind his floppy ears. He tolerated this with a look of bliss and some indecent moans and snuffles. When she abandoned him to turn to me, he settled at her feet with a sigh of satisfaction and buried his nose in his nether regions.

The dispatcher took down my story on a sticky note and punctuated it with two skeptical question marks. She told me all about the chief's family estate, just outside of town, a mansion only slightly falling down, a long line of town elders on his mother's side, stretching back and back, into the gravity of this northern place.

"I'm sure you'll be hearing from him soon," she said, almost coyly, as I tugged Rembrandt away from her dog-hair-adorned maroon tights. He pulled me down the sidewalk toward the scent of sourdough.

Despite the frigid air, the three fates huddled on their bench. "Got yourself a shiner," one of the old men mumbled.

"That's not a shiner, it's a goose egg," his neighbor scolded.

"Goosh egg," the third repeated, saluting me with his paper cup.

❄

The village cemetery reposed next to the ice rink, *state champions 1987, 1989, 1994*, across the street from the pizza parlor, *slice and wings $5.99*. Teenagers traversed it carrying duffel bags of sporting equipment, jingling quarters in their coat pockets. Cigarettes and condoms were plucked conscientiously by the village quilting club. The Boy Scout troop had mapped it in the seventies; the dead stretched back to 1766. I found five Janes and wrote their surnames down, my fingers numbing over the vowels. Two were infants who lived only a few days before going to ground. One of the child's tombs was guarded by a lamb. Its nose was black from rubbing, its hooves broken off. Of the remaining Janes, two were beloved mothers, one a devoted wife. Their gravestones were carved with stylized roses and angels, pared-down faces with ovoid eyes and rolls of hair. The bible passages had faded, but the bow lips and thorns had not.

❄

That night the police chief called as I was making dinner. Salads were my specialty. I chopped all the vegetables into identical ribbons. I tossed carrots to Rembrandt, who slobbered on them before spitting them under the counter. The chief asked if I'd seen a doctor, the concern in his voice like burnt sugar. "Just a scratch," I assured him, twisting the olive oil open one-handed. He said it was probably a runaway or a homeless person looking for food. The snow was starting up again; I heard the plow scrape its way up the hill in front of my house.

"Did you see anything at all?" he asked, and I could tell he doubted my story, wondered if my solitary life was getting the better of me. I beat the oil into the lemon juice vigorously. Emulsification takes some effort. Salt and pepper, splash of Tabasco, done.

❄

I took the scrap to the library and sat at a computer between an old lady ordering pre-packed bug-out bags and a kid playing Dungeons & Dragons online. I'd already searched the Internet at home and had come up with nothing substantive. The local newspaper and town records archives were equally unsatisfying. I had too little to work with. The name Jane was too common.

The local newspaper was kept on microfiche, rigid and chemical-smelling. I scanned the dates and names I'd gleaned from the tombstones. Nothing out of place; nothing that would account for a woman's death many decades later. It struck me that I'd never known a living Jane. Century-old days streamed past in yellow-tinted light. The machine whirred and clicked. A glass plate ground when I zoomed in. Advertisements for beard tonic and cocaine tooth drops came into focus. Mrs. Dwight Bellamy shared a recipe for pickled trout.

The microfiche machine was in a corner, behind a musty row of gardening books. The bookshelves in the library were mismatched, culled from donations, and this one exuded smells of cat piss and shaving cream. It was a veritable tour of the landscape, this library, the village encapsulated, bits and bobs from all the old homes, given over the years as charity or hubris, displayed haphazardly—a brass spittoon spouting a spider plant, dusty chandeliers with gaps of missing crystals, numerous framed samplers bedecking the walls, the stitched letters running amok, as if escaped from the volumes they hovered over. The library itself had once been a home and was still split into rooms, literature, nonfiction, and children's books each allotted their own chamber, mystery and romance lining the hallway that connected them. Harris's desk stood in the foyer, painted by the lavender and yellow stained glass in the front door. The desk and its accoutrements were solidly mid-fifties, burnished metal that evoked dreams of interplanetary travel. From my corner, I heard the old phone jangle and Harris's drawl. "Yes, she's here. No, not in the tower, down here. Sure thing, I'll keep an eye on her." A second later, his footsteps rounded the maze of bookshelves, and his white moustache floated into view. "Chief's a mite concerned about you," he said, eyes twinkling like a matchmaker's. "He's a hard case, that one, doesn't fluster easy, but here he is inquiring about your whereabouts."

"Maybe he suspects me of something." I wound the microfiche delicately back onto its reel, tucked it into the tattered cardboard box. The machine was hot enough to singe when I reached behind it for the off switch.

"Careful now," Harris called back over his shoulder as he trotted off to the kitchen and his unending supply of orange pekoe. I joined him at his desk just as the mugs came out and drank too quick, the tea scalding a line down my throat. So the police chief was worried for me.

Odd in such a cold place, how many things there were that burned.

✳

That night, working in the sun porch, I contemplated resurrection. In the Arctic, men died and rose again, years later, sailing back home on ships that had drifted free of the ice's clutch, health wrecked, remaining teeth jiggling in their sockets. Some men came back via the Inuit, sledged to civilization, wrapped in seal fur and the borrowed strength of the mother-wife they would never see again, fortified by soup flavored with the strong wild sage she had dried all summer while they had lain on pallets drawing maps, waxy muscles reknitting themselves. Is it any wonder I was still hoping for my family to return, somehow, in some form I might recognize? Claire was fickle, I told myself, changeable in a way that might allow her to pop up anywhere. But it was a lie. When it counted, she was ruthless, entirely committed. In our shared year of reckoning, commencing on our sixteenth birthday, she hadn't stopped at a kiss but had deflowered half the junior class and had the bouquet of tattooed initials to prove it. Each one a forget-me-not; I'd penned them for her with a needle sterilized over the candle and our father's India ink. She never flinched. My skin, though no less experienced, remained unmarked. I liked the small blows, the tattoo of typewriter keys. I remembered all too well without the needle.

❄

The encyclopedia items I was sent often fell under the heading of phenomena, for lack of a better term. Microscopic cold-hardy sea dwellers communicating through electric current, lichen blooms, the ways scurvy manifests, shifting glacial edges. Sometimes I wrote about stars. *Ursa Major*, loving mother nearly killed by her brave son, cast up to circle the pole forever as a bear, *Arktos*. Inside her gullet, an owl, a black hole. Sailors, cartographers, escaped slaves all held onto her tail because she never dipped below the horizon, though she came close enough in autumn to stain the trees with her blood. Strangely, though they were frozen, the things I wrote of seemed always in motion, transforming season to season, searching out new spaces: clouds of midges, bacteria markers tracing melt lines, all those frost-charred men in their canvas-winged caskets, flocks of terns, snow geese, tundra swans, stars loosening in their circuits, the migration of so many hearts, aloft.

❄

Finally I gave up on reason. I showed the scrap of letter to Harris. I proffered it to the old men outside the coffee shop, the goateed barista inside. At the post office, I slid it across the counter like an illicit message. The hairdresser fingered it under the spotless chandelier that dominated her shop. In the pizzeria, the teenagers snickered; at the hockey rink, the man driving the Zamboni lifted one muff of his ear protection and leaned across the ice. Everyone said it looked old. The police chief said, "How long have you had this?" I told him I found it in the woods. My woods were particularly fruitful that winter—who knew what else might turn up? I touched his forearm appealingly and shocked myself. He grinned, then scowled and sealed the bit of paper into a sandwich bag. "For testing," he said. "Though it is probably too late."

❋

Giving up that scrap of paper was like a feather lifting from the flock on my heart. I went home and collected Rembrandt, who had upset the canister of flour from the counter and was foaming white at the mouth. I wished there was somewhere I could go to drink grappa in a linen shift. I had mad ideas of returning to the police chief's office and undressing, peeling layers from myself like petal offerings. Instead, I wrapped my scarf around my throat more tightly and loaded the dog into the car. Attached to the gas station near the interstate was a Dunkin' Donuts, and I sat at the counter and sipped coffee with skim milk. Truck drivers and college students chatted around me. Rembrandt panted in the car. By the counter of the gas station was a display of souvenirs. Apples dangling from key chains and packets of pancake mix, resin moose and dead skyscrapers in globes of water. Outside, the snow fell as if the sky was molting. Everything smelled the chemical sweet of strawberry air freshener. The clerk wished a nice day on everyone, as if it were a curse.

❋

"Who did you show the evidence to?" the police chief asked when he called that night. I dissected artichoke hearts into half-buds and minced the anchovy fillets. The butcher, the baker, the candle-stick maker, I told him, feeling whimsical for once. "What did you tell them?"

He didn't mention dinner again; he didn't say his name. I'd put him in a compromised position. I explained that I'd said I found it while doing research for the encyclopedia entries I wrote. I told him about the Arctic collection at the library and he barked a laugh. "I know all about it," he said. The materials had belonged to his grand-father and his great-grandfather and his great-great-grandfather. His mother had donated them to the library.

"Then we have something in common," I said and smashed the cloves of garlic flat.

"Henna," he started, that dark sweetness back in his voice. A ra-dio crackled across the phone line. Mac McGregor was drunk again and trying to break into the convalescent home; the police chief had to go.

❄

The next day, the sun came out again for a few hours. False thaw. I buckled on my snowshoes. Rembrandt went howling into the woods. I hiked across Mariel's land to a ravine. Her hives were wrapped in black tarpaper and sat quiet. No one had fences here, though certain trees sported orange and yellow signs warning "Post-ed" and old barbed wire was grown into trunks. The stream flowed fast enough to avoid freezing completely, and I sidestepped down to it. The places that were under ice shimmered and bubbled. Dead leaves glowed at the bottom. There were no birds or insects. Deer had left trails on the banks.

Grief was a strange thing, not as constant as I'd imagined. But it had made me jumpy, suspicious, hard as a dried bean. Maybe I was fabricating a mystery where none existed because my back lot was easier to plumb than the ocean. Maybe the dead woman had just wandered away, had a streak of bad luck, let go of the thread. I understood transference, knew the temptation of twinning, but some part of me still wanted explanations, the whole story, preferably with a moral. Overhead, the sky stained blue as if drawing pleasure from the sunlight. I thought of the police chief's golden skin, and everything around me cracked.

❅

Back at my house, all the glass gleamed, reflecting white on blue on white, dazzling me so much that I nearly missed another scrap of paper, black bordered, fragile as a virgin's promise, pinned in the bare lilac bush that marked the edge of my yard, as if blown or perhaps snagged there as the woman was carried out of the woods. Only a partial date, *16, 1855*, in the same slanting hand, the same determined slash of ink.

TERRA INCOGNITA

O N THEIR WEDDING NIGHT, CAPTAIN Franklin drew down the shoulders of her dressing gown as delicately as he could. She was imperturbable in the drawing room, but here she trembled. His fingertips had been frozen and thawed so many times, barely any feeling remained in them. He imagined polar bears embracing, smelled the sharp tang of their meat. In the ice, men would eat anything raw. If a seal was shot, they fought over the musky liver. They licked the blood off their gloves. He twisted the knob of the lamp the wrong way and the gas hissed and flamed. Then he made it dark. The image of her he held in his mind was of her eyes widening, her nostrils flaring, sensing the hunt. He could plunge his hands into hot water and not flinch. But if he tried the experiment with ice water, his fingers burned unbearably.

Her skin was as fine as the satin she wore; they were indistinguishable. Beneath him, she seemed to be holding her breath. In the ice, there was nothing worse than the moment he blew out the lamp and the ship closed around his throat like a wooden collar. Everything constricting, the floes packing the ship, the bands of steel in the hull, the bookshelves lining the walls of the small cabin, the dead wool of his long underwear, tight from a monthly wash. She gasped beneath him and pulled him closer. The maps he drew had no edges; they stretched out and out into pure unknown space, into whiteness without end.

CHAPTER FIVE

T THE END OF THE week, I went back to the library, and Harris handed me the skeleton key. "I'm down here for a bit first," I said.

"The newspaper again?" Harris asked. "We should get you a velvet ribbon," he said, pointing to the coral cameo that swung from a chain at my throat. "Orange, I think," he laughed, poking fun at my sober attire. The necklace I'd picked up at an antique mall in Ohio on my drive across the country, part of my quest to acquire only memories that didn't belong to me, possessions that had no sting.

I added "1855" to "Jane" and "Bedford" and searched the catalogs of local documents again. Nothing. Harris hovered behind me. "Slow day?" I asked. The library sighed and the chandeliers tinkled softly as I broadened the search to include newspapers from the closest cities.

"Slow month," Harris said. "March is the burrowing time. People are hunkered down, just waiting now for a thaw." I glanced at the snow piled halfway up the downstairs windows. "Might have to wait a mite longer this year," Harris grimaced. "What have you got there?"

The old computer was clacking and whirring, spooling a list of results. The wife of a cobbler in Massachusetts, a child killed in a mine explosion, a slave who had found refuge with the Quakers. Nothing that seemed ripe for conspiracy a century and a half later.

"Still tracking down that bit of letter?" Harris sucked his teeth contemplatively. I didn't mention the second scrap. Harris had leaned over my shoulder and was poking at the keys. "1855, eh? Let's see. Crimean War, *Leaves of Grass* published, Exposition Universelle opened, Charlotte Brontë died." He tapped his fingers against his lips. "That was the year the old stone church steeple fell down, right in the middle of Sunday service, killed off an entire line of one of the town's founding families when it collapsed on their pew."

"How do you know that?" I rolled my shoulders, surprised.

"There's a plaque on the side of the church, see it every time I walk to work. Plus, Lucille Verney, she's the great-granddaughter of the man who repaired the steeple. She's old as dirt now, but still gets up every year during the village historical days and tells the story, scares the kiddies half to death."

"I don't think that's what I'm looking for."

"Know it when you see it, hmm?" He turned to straighten a stack of books, giving me a sidelong gaze. "The police chief's the one who knows all about the goings-on, back then and now. His mother donated that collection you're so fond of and is president of the ancestry committee, head of the preservation board. You should pay him a visit." That twinkle was back in his eye.

"Maybe," I said, remembering my impulse to present myself to the police chief, strip away my layers, and bask in his warmth. I wrapped my fingers around the skeleton key, hoisted my bag onto my shoulder, and headed for the narrow staircase almost hidden behind a carousel of horror paperbacks, all black and red and dripping roses. The stairs went up and up, past the three stories of the house that were no longer in use. Three floors of dead air relying on the shelves of books below as ballast to hold down the spidery old structure. Then a series of small leaded windows, the stairwell turning cylindrical, and the door that opened into the tower room, packed with musty volumes, old papers, decaying leather journals, a different world, a crow's nest facing north. When I went down to replace the key on its hook, Harris was gluing loan slips into the backs of books, a tub of paste at his elbow, his walrus moustache rather sticky.

"Everything all right up there?" he said. He held out my notebook, which I'd forgotten next to the computer with the new scrap of letter poking out like a bookmark. I resisted the urge to tuck it behind my back as I told him everything was dusty, cold, and quiet, just the way I liked it.

※

Back upstairs, I placed the piece of letter into the catchall of my doctor's bag, sandwiched between my passport and the map I'd picked up at the graveyard. Then I went over my checklist. My editor at the encyclopedia had sent me a packet of new names and places. Working with the collection was a challenge, since it was only partially catalogued. Pages of diaries were torn out, covers missing. Letters crumbled in their folios and the ink faded day by day. I opened the cover of one volume to find tiny parchment-colored creatures worming over the endpaper. Book lice. I set the book aside to be put in Harris's freezer for extermination and instead turned the pages of an account of an early overland expedition. A chart fell out. It was cracking where it had been folded, and I opened it gingerly. Across the top, *Snow Almanack* in ornate script, and a row of dates ran down the left edge, no years provided. The entries were numbered 119 through 130 and included inches measured, names of roads and towns, and in the last column, unexpected words, *honeysuckle, butter, wood rot, skunk*. I flipped the chart over and flecks of paper drifted onto the table. On the back, written in that same beautiful hand, was a note: *Thus completes my humble diary, for I am grown too old to tramp the fields and my senses are dulled by age. May those who come after me find some value in this document and let it stand a record of the miracles of nature and the Lord's goodness in all things. I leave the small cache I've*

*collected to my son for him to hopefully follow in my footsteps, may he
ever see them in the dark and day. And on this page, I adhere the last
flakes I gathered, that they might serve as remembrance of a life spent in
service of greater knowledge.* A series of splotches, like tear stains, dot-
ted the bottom of the page.

I was charmed by this oddity. Amidst all the dogged suffering of
the Arctic explorers, here was a person who so loved snow he recognized its various scents. In books, I'd read of children catching snowflakes on their tongues, though of course, this no longer was advised.
The writer seemed to have cultivated this same wonder. I tried to
imagine his 130 samples, the snow melted, latticework dispersed, a
collection relying on the resurrecting power of memory.

In my own work, hydrologists often kept libraries of water with
differing ionizations and salinity for reference. I had visited the archive in Illinois where vials were sent daily from all over the world
to be tested and catalogued, fed into updated risk models and live
supply maps. Those rooms filled with grids of uniform plastic tubes
hadn't sparked my affection the way this list had, with its grandiose
hopes. I wished I had the 130 jars before me, could imagine them
glinting in the winter light, corked, wax-capped, fragrance intact
in the trapped liquid, promise of honeysuckle and skunk, legacy of
miniscule desires.

I only hesitated a moment before carefully refolding the almanac
page and tucking it into my bag. Another small theft. Another partial document to anchor me here. Before long, I'd order a Peruvian
sweater. For now, work beckoned—yet another grim expedition. Ap-
pendages were frostbitten and thawed. The men drank their lime
juice in one swallow, with a grimace. They longed for the taste of
fresh meat, the saltiness of blood.

❄

Time passed in the tower room in thin rectangular shadows. The windows let in barely any light. My back was stiff by the time I heard Harris coming up the stairs to retrieve me, and I rose cautiously. The ladder let out a terrible screech as I pulled it down the row to reshelf the volumes. Harris's hand was on the doorknob. A key snicked in the lock and I turned to the door, puzzled. It should have already been unlocked. No one else had used the collection that day. No one ever did.

I flew to the door and twisted the knob. It did not give. "Harris," I called, and no one answered. How stupid to be locked in by mistake. "Harris," I shouted.

Just then, the one inadequate fluorescent tube and the desk lamp went out. But how could Harris already be downstairs flipping the breaker to close up? The flight of stairs to the tower was long and arduous, impossible to navigate so quickly. So, not a mistake then. Someone other than Harris had turned the lock. I cried out and pounded on the door, for a moment forgetting myself, feeling the dark tower walls closing in. Then I pressed my face to the cold wood and was calm. There was nothing to be done.

I stayed there with my head against the door, thinking that I really needed to purchase a flashlight, when a sliver of terror pierced my heart. Something white had appeared at my feet with a whisper. It was a sheet of paper, slid under the door. I didn't dare move. Someone had listened to me cry out and had done nothing. Then I realized how ridiculous I was; of course my tormentor hadn't freed me. He or she had trapped me here. I picked up the paper and retreated to the farthest point from the entry, half behind the edge of a bookcase.

"Let the dead rest," the note read, just like in some cut-rate thriller, block letters legible even in the fading light.

❄

I broke then, I will admit. I took up my notebook and tore the blank pages from the end. Even in my panic, I was conscious of the work I'd done, protective of my investments. Panting, I dragged the bookcase ladder to the farthest end of its rail, all the while thinking of the person lurking behind the tower door, key in hand, and the coming dark. Harris wouldn't come to look for me. Many times before, I'd slipped out when he was deep in story hour. When I hadn't come down at the signal of the lights switching off, he would have never guessed I was locked up here.

The casement window was hard to open. I broke my fingernails down to the quick. Blood made the handle slippery, but finally it gave a bit, enough for me to shove the pages through. The window was too high; I could not see where they landed, but I imagined them sifting like snowflakes to the sidewalk below. Too late, I realized I should have written messages. I was too tired to eviscerate my notebook further. The top of the ladder seemed the safest place in the room, the farthest away from the door and whatever waited behind it. So I clung to the rungs, straining toward the crack of the open window, unsure whether the rustlings I heard were something moving in the darkness or the manuscripts that circled me recoiling from the fresh air.

❄

That night, at dinner, village children reported there were ghosts in the library tower.

❄

"What did you think would happen?" the police chief said when he unlocked the door. By that time, I had regained my composure and was seated properly at the large oak table, my only concession to my predicament the long hooked staff I held across my lap. I'd found it tucked behind one of the bookshelves and recognized it as a tool to open the transom above the interior door. I did not open that window because I could not see how it would help my cause, but the staff itself, with its blunt cast-iron implement, seemed a good weapon, especially when my other choices were moldy ship's logs and brittle maps.

By the time the police chief and his man came to release me, it was full dark and I had resigned myself to spending the night there. I had thought of the destruction Rembrandt would wreak on the living room; I had contemplated the impossibility of sleeping on a pallet made of geological treatises. Mostly, I had listened to those lost explorers coming alive in the dark, murmuring to each other, moaning over their wounds and empty bellies, their blackened forms scuttling around me, hungry for sensation.

❄

The officer could not stop talking. It was the same one from before, the one with the red ears. He called me "ma'am" with a kind of awe. I was the most exciting thing to happen to this village in some time. He loped about, trailing fingerprint powder over every-thing, sneezing and whooping, muttering about logistics. He asked me again and again what time I'd been shut in, told the story of Dolly Singh from a few houses down who'd convinced her parents there really was something trapped in the library tower. Finally, the police chief sent him away, down to the basement to flip the breaker.

The police chief stood close to me so I could see him in the sips of light from the windows. He said, "Weren't you hoping to stir something up?" His hair was even more gilded in the moonlight, but the lower part of his face was cloaked, darkened by stubble and shadow. His hands clutched at my shoulders as he shook me once and drew me toward him. The scent of steel and caramel encircled me. Then the fluorescent tube buzzed on and he stepped back. I straightened my collar and stared levelly at him. His tenderness was the least likely thing to break my composure at this point.

"We should have dinner some night," he said, and I moved my head slightly. It might have been a nod.

❋

When I arrived home, I found Rembrandt had chewed the newspaper and left it in messy clumps on the sofa. The print had bled into the fabric, leaving great grey blossoms on the flaxseed. I let him out and heard him tear off into the woods. After he returned, I sat in the sun porch, lights off, watching the shadows on the snow. I was too excited to sleep. The night's events had proven one thing: the woman in my backyard had been no accident. There was some secret meaning to her death, a plot I could unravel, if I just knew where to start.

DIP NEEDLE

*T*HE MEN AROUND THE TABLE asked what walrus tasted like, and what about lichen and moose? One man, to whom he had not been introduced, asked in a daring tone about dog meat. Captain Franklin said nothing. It would not do to tell them that once your gums started decaying from lack of fresh food, everything tasted of copper.

The Raleigh Travellers' Club met twice a month to eat a meal inspired by a member's travels. Contrary to the fact of Captain Franklin's presence, the theme of the day was not the Arctic, but rather Russia. There was a vast array of soups—fish stew, cabbage broth, a concoction of sour milk and boiled pork, served cold. Footmen proffered dishes of dumplings, some filled with potato, some with cherries. A large platter of *blini* arrived last, ringed with caviar and sour cream, crepes thin as compliments, melting on the tongue.

Captain Franklin retreated to a corner, feeling the habitual pangs of indigestion. A soft-faced man in a brown suit sidled up to him. The man wondered if the captain might gather a sample for him on his next journey. Just one small vial of northernmost snow would be worth a great deal to him. The captain could name his price. Captain Franklin felt groggy from the vodka and the late nights squiring his new wife to various salons. He suspected a hoax. Was this the man who had asked about the dogs? Out on the ice, it was an act of discipline to stay upright. In the hot dining room, he grabbed at the arm of a passing servant and thus was towed into the entrance hall, away from the chattering men and their delicacies, their bizarre imaginations.

A mile away, his wife was a slender spire, still opaque to him. His inclination drew him through the London streets. No need for a hack, walking was a pleasure over such solid pavement, and he wanted to savor the space between them, the shivery promise of discovery.

CHAPTER SIX

*T*HE SKY KEPT FALLING. I hadn't seen green in months. The wind chill siren howled up from the village. The snowplow dragged its bag of bones over the pavement all night. The salt ration was depleted, so they spread ashes instead. Rembrandt dove into the white, disappeared, reappeared. Cold snap. Every faucet in the house dripped to keep the pipes from freezing. The ozone layer was clumping up in some places, shredding in others. I had to remind myself that two-thirds of the children on the planet had never seen an ice cube. At fifteen below zero, my lungs whiskered with frost. Even the old timers stayed in, and the world spun its own fate, cloud patterns and jet streams, ruts of frigid air, the breath of dying places.

❄

The police chief took me to a French restaurant two villages to the east. The dispatcher's brother owned it. We parked in front of the drugstore where an old woman stood in the window, dangling plastic eggs on a tree made of wire hangers. I wore my highest-necked blouse with a paper-thin cardigan and military-style jacket buttoned over it, and scarf and hat and gloves and two pairs of tights under my knee-length skirt, and boots that laced the length of my calves. All black, of course. The police chief wore a sports coat, an oxford shirt fraying at the collar, faded jeans, and a grin.

To get inside the restaurant, we had to make our way through a small maze of velvet curtains designed to keep out the chill. The establishment consisted of two tables and a purple door, presumably to the kitchen. One table held a fishbowl filled with darting silver. We chose the other. A girl, no more than twelve years old, came through the purple door bearing two glasses of red wine. The police chief leaned back in his chair and said for the third time, "Call me Fletcher."

❄

No menu appeared. Nor did any French food. The child brought us saucers of slivered raw beef, a peony of flesh, then violet-brown chicken livers in a bowl, and then two steaks, sprawled in pools of blood. She refilled our wine glasses like an automaton, not one drop spilled. The room was staining red. Fletcher leaned across the meats and my stomach clenched. He wiped the corner of my mouth with his thumb and it came away looking like I had bitten it, smeared carmine.

"So, you're playing detective," he chided. He told me stories of his ancestor who fought in the War for Independence, the Revolutionary War, he amended, and came home crazy, sliced up one of the servants to see the hidden parts. "Curiosity," he said, "can be unhealthy."

At the other table, the silver shifted. I watched the light play on his hair and felt that old rush of the wave rising beneath me. He reached across the table again, this time for my hand, and the room blushed hotter. He said he knew about my family. He didn't say he was sorry, for which I was grateful; all those apologies I had endured had only hardened my shell. Instead, there was a wry sort of knowledge in his beautiful voice, almost a mocking tone. I liked how sharp he made me feel, as if I were touching things with my bare skin.

For dessert, a plate of rabbits' hearts, each more tender than the last.

❄

At my door, Fletcher released his grip on my arm so I could fit the key to the lock. The walk was icy. "Want me to come in, to make sure nothing else has happened?" His cotton shirt fell open at the throat. He would be so easy to undress. I would be more difficult.

One kiss. I leaned into him, off the spikes of my heels. Warm air trickled from the doorway. He tasted of the ocean—metal and decay—and that undertone of burnt sugar. I drank him in, and everything inside me flared. For a moment, I felt all the buried tributaries rushing. And then I slipped inside and closed the door. The heat spilled over me, all the sweeter for the knowledge of the cold outside.

❄

That night, I dreamed again of Claire, a happy dream, and woke up laughing in the dead dark, my pillow wet with tears. She'd said she had a secret, a fine joke. She'd leaned in to whisper it to me, her breath a paintbrush on my cheek. Someone had killed that woman. Even if they hadn't wrapped their hands around her throat, they had driven her outside into the snow, barefoot, bareheaded, wearing next to nothing. Murder. And yet, this was a small town, *a village*, as the sign said. The houses around me were far flung, but not impossibly so. Why hadn't she knocked on someone's door—why hadn't she knocked on *my* door? What had been done to the dead woman before she went out into the night? Who had chased her? In this part of the world, no one wandered around barefoot in January, not even the demented ones, the old ladies in the nursing home who sang scales all day and had to be locked up so they didn't drift away.

❄

The morning after dinner with Fletcher, the temperature soared and brought a warm snow, big languorous flakes that floated like moths in the air. I made coffee in the French press, bearing down on the grounds, scalding my fingers on the stainless steel bands around the glass. All this snow was making my heart break a little. I missed my sister. I wished she could have been there beside me, eating the top of her muffin first, pouring too much sugar into her cup. "Idiot," she would say, and ask why I hadn't invited Fletcher in, plied him with whisky and digitized torch singers, thrown him onto my bed and ravished him until the sun rose. "Any port in a storm," she would say. Claire was always the one in danger of sinking, the moody and dear one, the impulsive one, the one everyone asked to parties even knowing she would bring me along. She had a tattoo of the North Star on her wrist and never wore a watch. Her books were organized by color and she kept epoxy next to the boxes of rice in her cupboard. And none of it had helped.

Rembrandt snuffled my leg and laid his warty head on my foot. "Okay," I said, and went for my snowshoes, the leash, a bottle of water, three dog biscuits, silk long underwear, fleece tights, fleece sweater, wool socks, sheepskin-lined boots, down vest, hat, gloves, scarf, sunglasses. I felt like there was something I was forgetting.

❄

Once outside, I headed for the hawthorn bush like a needle that had been magnetized. Rembrandt was curiously subdued. The snow fell around us like a veil. Wedding snow, the kind that sticks to your eyelashes. I hiked uphill and then down into a small ravine. Nothing moved except us. Back uphill and my hamstrings burned. Too many days in front of the typewriter. The new words my editor had sent me were stones in my pocket. *Terra incognita, ice blink, permafrost.* Something to keep me from floating away into the snow.

At the top of the hill, Rembrandt dove away into the woods. I pulled off my hat and scarf, and the sky fell on my head. Sweet Claire, gone to water. Love of my life, my better half; all those terms used for marriage could have applied to us. We were two ends of a circuit. And now, there was a piece of myself I could never turn off, a nagging awareness, a small ache in my liver, always burning.

Rembrandt reappeared, dragging something with his mouth. I dreaded seeing what he had found. He cast it at my feet proudly and then flopped down to gnaw at it. Deer leg, just the foreleg and the hoof. I wrenched it from him and threw it into the ravine behind us, grabbed him by the collar and pulled him along, not surprised when he snarled and loped off. Alone, I made my way to the back edge of my property, where the hawthorn stood like a crown in the snow, inviolate, its branches spiked with shrouded thorns.

❄

Under the hawthorn, the snow was clear. No trace of any disturbance. I held my breath. The tree branches knocked into each other. A squirrel chattered. Far away, cars murmured on the highway. Water was trickling somewhere. Again, I had the feeling of being watched. The sky was perfectly colorless, and the snow fell faster. Why had the woman ended here? The woods formed an inflated, swooping S on the county map, dipping in and out of a steep ravine to sputter out on my land.

I started to move further into the trees, in a direction the woman might have come from. Something slammed into the backs of my knees and my breath whooshed out as I dropped forward into the snow. Rembrandt snuffled at me, nudging my chin in apology. Then he lifted his head and growled, the fur standing up on his neck as he stared into the forest. I lay quiescent for a moment, waiting, but nothing happened. The woods were silent but for Rembrandt's growling. There was no way to rise gracefully in snowshoes, but I scrambled to my feet, wondering what might come next. The pines stood dark as secrets; it took all my will to turn my back on them and head for Mariel's.

She was tucked into her still room, the pantry where she jarred the honey and made the candles and tinctures she sold online. Light flooded through an arched, multi-paned window, and the walls were lined with shelves holding packets of crushed herbs and great globes of honey. The floor was painted blue, and in the corner was a tiny woodstove, hive-shaped and enameled yellow. She was dipping tapers, lowering the wicks with their penny weights into an aluminum pot and then plunging them into ice water. The smell of beeswax filled the room.

Midway through our conversation, she dug into the pocket of her white linen apron and pulled out a card, prewritten. *The hermit has emerged!* The hermit was a mysterious creature, a newcomer like me, a man who had rented the Vanderkey house for the winter while its owners sheltered in Florida. The house perched on the hill opposite ours, across the ravine, and on clear nights, with the leaves off the trees, we could occasionally spy a light in the windows. But the inhabitant himself had not been seen. There was some debate in the village as to whether he had ever actually taken up residence. I asked Mariel how she knew he'd surfaced. She tapped her ear vigorously, setting her silver earrings chiming, wrote, *the bees gossip*, and presented it to me with a grin.

When I went down to the village for Rembrandt's sourdough, the old men had resumed their positions in front of the bakery. They were wrapped in layers of flannel and wool, all with caps advertising various farm equipment in lieu of winter hats. It seemed spring was around the corner. The old men greeted me with an exuberance that made me fear they had heard about my date with Fletcher, but instead they wanted to talk about the hermit.

"Fine fellow," they said. "Name of Plother."

"No, Proffer."

"Prufer."

"Had on a tie that would blind you," they cackled. Rembrandt nudged me toward the bakery door.

❄

That evening, I played a game Claire and I had made up. I squeezed the pips from a lemon and sucked the bitterness away. Nine blonde seeds on the tabletop. To perform a séance, you needed an odd number. I lit candles, left the door to the sunroom open so the draft came in to make them dance. What Claire and I had constructed so long ago, on new moon nights while our parents drank wine in the studio, wasn't a summoning but a projection. Nine planes flew overhead in the dark sky, packed with skin and bones. Nine whales spun in the thick sea. Nine semi-trucks slept on the highway to the west. Nine houses glowed in a gold line down the hill. Nine turtle shells were buried in Mariel's yard. Nine conchs served as their gravestones. Nine wishes buzzed round my head. The pips on the table shivered out of their circle and the magic broke. The world went random again, Rembrandt burped in his sleep, and I swept the spent seeds into my palm and tossed them out into the snow, where they sank, tiny shipwrecks.

ICE BLINK

ARRIAGE BROUGHT HER MANY THINGS—A title, a step-daughter, the freedom to travel. She took an iron bed-stead everywhere she went. She had two servants to carry it. The bed went to Egypt, to Alaska, to Hawaii, to Japan. It was sized for one. In Egypt, she visited the Temple of Isis, winged goddess, protector of the dead, whose name meant "throne," who married her brother and, when he was killed, searched the world for his pieces, hunted every single scrap to bring him back to life. The parallels to her own fate were not yet clear, but she loved the faceless lions at the entrance, unrelenting in their mission.

At Isis's temple, the wind was so bad that she tore a portion of her skirt to wrap around her face. A fellow traveler—a European missionary her own age, browned and handsome, flopping lock of hair over the brow, white laugh lines around his eyes—pulled her into a shady space out of the dust storm. Her eyes and mouth were filled with grit and he washed them gently with the tepid water of his canteen. Her husband sailed somewhere south of them, crisscrossing the Mediterranean at the whims of the Admiralty. His bones were not yet scattered. She was free to let the warm water pool in her mouth. When she spat it, the ground absorbed it instantly.

A similarity between the desert and her husband's frozen expanses—the possibility for mirage. Jane indulged it, let her eyes drift to the horizon, spied a parasol, a narwhal tusk, the shape of a man, striding toward her.

CHAPTER SEVEN

EVERAL PEACEFUL DAYS WENT BY. No one attacked me. No one tried to kiss me. Rembrandt sighed mournfully and chewed up a whole box of blue envelopes. I worked in the library tower, always with the door propped open a bit. In the streambeds and the catch ponds, the water was rising. I could feel the tingle in my hands and feet. I'd been a talented dowser before my family disappeared; it was almost painful, the hope that welled in me when I thought of being able to dowse again. "Want to practice?" I asked Rembrandt one day, and he lumbered to the door.

❖

Once outside, he was a different dog, nipping at the air, poking his nose in piles of questionable substances. Snow still spread around us, but the air was mild and small birds hopped from tree to tree. Dowsing is mostly just paying attention to the signs, declivities in the landscape, clustering of plants, animal burrows, wind patterns. The hard part is the part that is inexplicable, the *feeling* of water, sensing it circulating deep underground. Even still water has a current, much like a wire carrying electricity. This is its signature and its force. The vibration is so slight and so much a part of our usual background noise that most people can't feel it without a tool to convey it. Most dowsers use a stick or wand or something living. Doves are good, as are snakes. One of my former colleagues carried a toad in a cage of gold mesh. I was rather unique, and the subject of much consternation in graduate school, in using myself as the conduit. One old professor, bearded, creases like scars on his forehead, argued that theoretically my very blood could boil if the currents attained resonance. It is true that in the lab, once in a while, a salamander or a chickadee would explode. But I was a much larger system of veins and intersections. When I dowsed with my blood, it felt cold, not hot. It was a chill that spread upward from my feet to my scalp, slowing my breath. I hadn't felt it in so long, I wondered if I'd be able to control it.

❅

Even under the best of circumstances, it was difficult to dowse in winter. The whispers of the snow muddled things. Though it was a warm day, the ground was still mostly frozen. I had to go deep.

I stood still for a long time, remembering the feel of water. The birds began to sing again. My shins numbed, then my kneecaps. All my blood was drawing up, into the loose fist of my heart.

❅

If I were not careful, even my heart would chill and slow, winding down, wringing the liquid from my body. Maybe that is what began to happen; when Rembrandt came through the woods and leapt onto me, knocking me over, I sat up to find I had tears in my eyes. He snuffled at me and something dropped from his mouth, a scrap of brittle paper, the handwriting familiar by now.

"Where did you find it?" I asked him, and placed my hand on his collar. I had my doubts about following Rembrandt into the woods, but I did it anyway, the scrap of paper tucked into my pocket. Around us, the bare trees mixed with the dead, their slender trunks thrusting up like the masts of a hundred ships buried in the snow. My legs were still unsteady, but I could feel the water now, the great relief of it, running sluggishly far beneath us, beating through the earth.

❄

The sun was bright and everything glittered. The next scrap of letter I found snagged on a branch about chest high. The next was down low, perched in a clump of weeds thick with burrs. I came up with my gloves covered in the spiky wheels, and only had a chance to glance at the paper before I noticed the birds had stopped singing and Rembrandt had disappeared. *Abandoned*, I thought just as I heard him crashing back toward me through the undergrowth. Hoping to beat him at his own game, I ducked behind an old oak, its grey bark as scarred as any river. When the rustling was quite close, I jumped out. But it was a man standing there, dark figure in a dark jacket, arms outstretched.

❄

"Careful," Fletcher said, catching me by my elbows.

I gasped, trying to find my breath. "What are you doing out here?"

"Technically, this is my land," he said with a satisfied grin. The smile dropped away when he saw what I was clutching. "What's this?" he said and plucked it from me, quick as a flame. After one look, he sighed and slipped it into his pocket. "Henna," he said. "What am I going to do with you?"

The tenderness in his voice had me leaning toward him. Then he took my empty hand and drew the glove off, finger by finger. His hands were already bare. Carefully, silently, he picked the burrs from my glove, then repeated the service for the other one. He held both gloves in one of his fists and looked steadily at me. On the ground around him, the fallen discs of the burrs formed a pattern I couldn't discern. I felt my waterlogged heart releasing and all of my blood flowed simultaneously into my veins, out and back again, out and back.

"Henna," he repeated and stepped forward, his free hand going to the base of my throat, the pulse that beat there. And then his lips were on mine and they tasted of metal and earth and dark things. I thought of the animals combusting in the lab. His fingers gripped my jaw. My gloves dropped away and I stumbled back into the rough bark of the oak. The two of us cast one shadow on the snow, a wash of perfect blue.

❋

He walked me home through the woods, his palm a wedge at the small of my back. He gave me a lecture about the bit of letter he'd plucked from me, and though I enjoyed his concern, I didn't tell him about the other two scraps safe in my pocket. It had been so long since someone worried over me, but I wasn't quite ready to divulge all. True, he was rakishly handsome, and good by all accounts, the defender of the village, savior of drunks and old ladies, rescuer of stranded motorists and displaced bodies. I was out of practice, but my cells strained toward him, a frisson of electricity much like the call of buried water. It occurred to me that the return of my dowsing coincided with him.

I had gotten used to being solitary, even reveled in it, but I could feel myself surfacing, growing attentive. Rembrandt jumped out at us from the very last tree before my yard. Fletcher spun as the dog leapt and growled at him, an instinctive feral sound from down deep in his chest. He cuffed the dog roughly behind the ear, sweeping him away from us. "Sorry," Fletcher said to me, with a grimace, reaching out to touch a lock of hair that had escaped from my hat. "Police reflexes." Rembrandt, unperturbed, ambled toward the back door.

The sky went grey in an instant, the sun gone over the far hills. At the door, Fletcher didn't say anything, just held out his hand for the key.

❄

While I was chopping the fennel, Fletcher opened the wine, the tendons of his wrist flexing. I tore bread into hunks, sliced tender mozzarella. Everything on the plate was white; the wine was gold. It clung in my throat like honey. For dessert, one pear, halved, eaten by candlelight. The snow started falling again, forming a screen around the house.

"Why the Arctic?" Fletcher asked.

"I wanted the cold," I said. "And the library's collection…your collection." I touched his wrist briefly. "The materials are convenient."

"Pragmatic," he said, and laughed. He had a beautiful laugh, rich as treacle; it made the room glow until my cheeks heated.

"What about your grandfathers? Why all the Arctic materials?"

Fletcher leaned back in his chair, stretching lazily, those lovely biceps bunching. "My maternal great-grandfather and his father and his father before him worked for the Hudson's Bay Company. They dabbled in shipping even though they ended up landlocked here. Originally, they were from Montreal, and they were…" He paused for a moment, searching for the word. "Collectors, I guess you'd call them."

"And your father's family?"

"Glovemakers," he said, and reached again for my hand.

❄

His kisses raised goosebumps along the inside of my arm. His head was bent, but I had the sense he was smiling. His hair brushed against the side of my breast and I shivered. When he started to unbutton my shirt, I caught his strong wrist. As I had imagined, he was easier to undress. Myself, I wanted to keep some layers, some of that reserve I'd built up over the last eighteen months. He clasped me to him and we drowned together, his skin rough against my few exposed parts. I sank myself into him, his clever hands, the strong bellows of his lungs, and I was almost warm there.

Afterward, he tried again to unclothe me, seemed to be settling in for the night. "Too fast," I whispered. I thought I caught a flash of exasperation and then he raised my fingertips to his lips, grimaced ruefully and said, "Why, look at the time." He refused a ride home. At the door, booted and zipped into his heavy jacket, wool hat pulled down to his eyes, he reached for me again, held my head in both of his large hands, and kissed me hard. For an instant I felt teeth, and then he released me and stepped back. "Lock the door, Henna," he said as he walked out into the dark.

I thought of the scraps of letter in my coat pocket. I left them there. My brain felt fogged and I wanted to luxuriate in it, give up the dead to their own devices for one night.

❄

Mariel placed the cups of tea on the table and sat down across from me. We breathed in the steam for a moment. Moonflower and elderberry, vanilla and thyme.

Love or Lust? Mariel scrawled in silver.

"Neither," I said, waving away the steam between us. "I don't know."

Lust, then, Mariel wrote and capped the pen. We sipped in silence, watching the ever-present snow float past the window.

"What do bees do in spring?" I asked.

Brood, Mariel wrote, and then she laughed—the whine of a saw catching on the trunk of a tree. I laughed with her, and so did the bees far away in their hives, slumbering still, shivering with mirth.

❄

I worked all day, typing out entry after entry. The black letters floated around me, buzzing, snowflakes in negative.

I imagined them, the men in their ships, swinging thigh to thigh in their hammocks, packed tight as bees. The captain their queen. All of them waiting.

Once my fingers were warm enough from typing, I got the scraps of letter from my jacket pocket and laid them on a blank sheet of paper. Carefully, I wrote in the text from the piece I had relinquished to Fletcher. They read: *My husband, missing but not forgotten* and *Time has come to take more decisive action* and *Hope I can rely upon your discretion and loyalty and your undying love of those polar regions, so dear, too, to his noble heart.*

❄

It was becoming clearer, though no more likely than any other of the events this long winter. At the library, I pulled the squealing ladder to the farthest corner. Up top, tucked away between larger volumes, was a small book bound in blue cloth, cover embossed in gold script. *Portrait of Lady Franklin.* When I opened it, standing there on the ladder, the spine creaked, exhaling the smell of tea leaves and rain-soaked pavement.

❄

Lady Jane Franklin, wife of Sir John Franklin, one of the most famous Arctic explorers in history. Famous not for his discoveries but for his disappearance. In 1845, with HMS *Terror* and HMS *Erebus*, he sailed with 128 men in search of the Northwest Passage, and none of them were seen alive again. I climbed down from the ladder and

seated myself at the long oak table. The radiators clanged as if herald-
ing my much-delayed perception.

Franklin was never found, despite dozens of expeditions being
sent after him. Nearly ten years later, the skeletons of some of his
crew would be discovered strewn across King William Island, fleeing
their ice-locked ship after years of entrapment, suffering from starva-
tion, marks of butchering upon their bones. And a few years after
that, a note was found declaring Franklin dead just two years into
the journey, his post taken over by his second-in-command who, in
1848, a year after the captain's death, fled the ships with the remaining men in desperate search of food and shelter.

In the decades that followed, dozens of expeditions set forth,
even into the very recent past, when scholars still debated the location of the ships, sent scientists to uncover bodies from cairns to
investigate the possibility of botulism, of lead poisoning from the
newfangled tin cans. And then, in 2014 and 2016, after a century
and a half of searching, both ships were finally found, submerged
in shallow icy water: HMS *Terror* in Terror Bay south of King William Island and Franklin's flagship, HMS *Erebus*, south of Victoria
Island. I'd seen the footage on the Internet of their encrusted hulls
and splintered planks burnished bronze by the sonar imaging and the
video from the remote dive vehicle, panning the barnacle-adorned
Erebus, so perfectly preserved by the cold water that glass was still in
the portholes.

❋

Harris called up the staircase to invite me to tea. Since being
locked in the tower, I was allowed to keep the key with me as I
worked, even though there was no spare. When I came down to the
foyer, I was surprised to see an unfamiliar man sitting at Harris's
desk, fussily arranging the three tea cups on saucers and portioning

out the vanilla wafers. Harris emerged from the kitchen carrying a small jug of milk and a cup heaped with sugar cubes, a formality he didn't bother with when it was just the two of us.

"Henna, did you meet Mr. Plover?"

The little man rose from behind the desk, rotund and beaming, and extended his hand. He was wearing a violently purple suit, a yellow shirt, and a tie blazoned with oversized poppies. A wing of artificially black hair folded over his pate. This had to be the hermit, inappropriate as our nickname seemed now. His hand was damply warm, and he shook vigorously as if wringing the neck of something. His smile never faltered all through our tea as he expounded on a variety of subjects, everything from the genealogical history of the area to the cost of milk in the early twentieth century and the relation of advances in transportation to the demise of the small farm. He seemed to know a lot about black flies and tree sap. He spent fifteen minutes on the intricacies of mummification. Of particular interest to him was the rate of cooling of the lava of Mount Vesuvius, and he was hoping to find this information in the library's stacks, along with an inventory of the La Brea Tar Pits. I was ready to escape back to the peace of the tower before my cup was half empty, but Harris was invigorated, his moustache twitching at each change of topic, his eyes darting from shelf to shelf as if mentally marking the books he would proffer.

As I took my leave, Mr. Plover produced a business card with the flourish of a magician. It was heavy cream stock, letterpressed elegantly with *C. C. Plover* and below that, in large curlicued script, *The Extinction Museum.* Back in the tower, I slipped the card into my bag. It weighed no more than the other things I'd collected that winter, but it bothered me, and I resolved to look up Mr. Plover and his enterprise when I was back home. For the time being, I returned to that famous lost expedition and the flocks of explorers that followed the *Erebus* and the *Terror* into the unmapped ice.

Lady Jane Franklin had sown the kernels of polar fervor in the years she spent exhorting the Admiralty and wealthy American capitalists to send ships into the North, looking for her husband. She was inexhaustible, well-informed, connected like a spider in a web to national heroes, wealthy businessmen, politicians, and writers. Charles Dickens took up her cause. Disraeli was a family friend. I refreshed my memory of her iron will as I skimmed the butter-colored pages of the old book. The heat had set the packets of paper round the room fluttering. The radiators clicked off and cold oozed in around my feet.

The last chapter began with a list of numbers. From 1848 to 1859, thirty-five expeditions set off in search of Franklin, eleven of which were directly funded or arranged by Jane Franklin. For fourteen years, a woman had essentially commanded the ships of two nations; she had suggested routes and corresponded tirelessly, opening the Northwest Passage from afar. Her slight biography noted that over her long life she had filled dozens of journals, written innumerable letters. But how had one of them ended up in the hand of a dead woman in my woods?

MIGRATION

*J*ANE'S HUSBAND REQUIRED CONSTANT PRODDING, even after he disappeared. Fortunately, she enjoyed maneuvering, letter writing, nation-building over tea. Her misfortune was that she was quicker than most men and not afraid to show it. Perpetually frustrated, she spread her ambitions farther, reminded her husband ice was his destiny, helped him woo the Admiralty into a new commission, stitched the Union Jack in silk and draped it over him while he was napping away his last afternoon at home. Shocked to wake a corpse, he yelled at her for the only time in their marriage. The next day he set sail, bound for darkness, mollified by the good omen of a dove on the mast of his ship, never knowing she had paid for three dozen of them to be released on the docks that morning.

CHAPTER EIGHT

*M*Y HEAD THROBBED AS I locked the tower room and started downstairs. I couldn't quite make sense of the connections. How did a woman carrying pieces of a letter that should have been tucked away in an acid-free folder in some climate-controlled collection turn up dead in the backyard of the one person in town who might recognize the importance of that object? Her face flashed in my mind again, but I still felt no glimmer of recognition.

Of course, there was another person in town who would know the value of that letter.

❋

Fletcher leaned against the wall next to the desk, talking basketball with Harris. When he saw me, he pushed himself upright, one lock of golden hair falling boyishly over his forehead. His strong, even teeth gleamed at me. "Carry your books?" he said, gesturing toward the bulging doctor's bag. Without waiting for an answer, he slipped the leather strap from my wrist and clamped his other hand over the soreness there, steering me toward the door.

"My place," he said, pointing us toward the police station. The sidewalks were crusted with ice and grime. The snow stung our faces. My breath came quick. His mouth was grim as he ushered me toward his office; he wasn't allowing for any demurrals today. Somehow, he must know about the other fragments of the letter, folded away in the bag he was gripping.

❄

When I was in school, all the girls had mandatory weekly self-defense class from the first grade on. The only time it was canceled was once in fourth grade, when we ate pink cakes and watched a film about getting our periods instead. After that, we had self-defense class every day, after lunch, while the boys read Shakespeare. We got to choose our style of fighting. Claire picked sparrow style, which involved a lot of hopping around and high-pitched screams. Our best friend, Ethel, practiced revulsion techniques such as eating grass to induce vomiting and talking about dental hygiene. After much thought, I had chosen misdirection.

❄

I had a lot of practice slipping. And the walk was icy. Fletcher caught me before I fell, staggered back, and then held me around the waist tightly until I righted myself. I leaned closer to him, tasted his jaw. Brine and lime blossom. "Too fast," he said, setting me away from him as he glanced up and down the street. Inside the police office, the dispatcher peered at us and smiled from behind a thicket of tattered Valentine's cards.

❄

I sat in the suspect's seat in his office. The smell of mildew wafted around me. Fletcher rested his hips on the edge of his desk, his knee brushing my knee. "We've discovered the identity of the woman on your property," he said, leaning toward me. The blood rushed to my cheeks. "She was a doctoral candidate in history at the University of

New Hampshire. She was doing research on Sir John Franklin." He cocked his head at me to see if I recognized the explorer's name. I nodded at him impatiently. "Apparently she had found a letter in the library's special collections she thought was important, and for some reason she decided to bring it to me."

"To you?" I blurted.

"You sound surprised," he said with a smile, as if this were some party game we were playing.

"But why you?"

"She was deranged, obviously." Fletcher impatiently pushed the hair back from his forehead, and I saw the lines of worry there. For a man used to protecting everyone, he must have hated this woman dying en route to him, practically on his land. "My family's collection has a very minor reputation, a few footnotes here and there." Pride threaded the exasperation in his voice. "She must have run across it somehow, stole that letter from the archive, and drove out here, it seems, though we still haven't located her car. She probably went off the road somewhere up by the ravine and spent the night wandering the woods. Why she wasn't wearing shoes or a coat, we'll never know," he said, shaking his head brusquely, professional demeanor restored.

"But why is the letter in pieces? Was it that way in the archive?"

"You've only found two pieces, right?" He arched an eyebrow at me. I held very still, being sure not to look at my bag. "The rest of the letter may be intact. The library hadn't scanned that document, so they simply have a number for it and the knowledge that it is missing."

"But why was she carrying it with her? Why not leave it in the car? They don't have a record of whom the letter was from? Or to?"

"Henna," he said, and took my hand. My fingers were ice against his warm skin. He ducked his head to blow on them, and for a moment, I thought I saw his police chief's mask fall again, a furrow appearing between his eyebrows, a wince as if in pain. "We don't know what she was thinking, and it's no use torturing ourselves. I'm sure her car will turn up soon and maybe we will learn more, but until then..." He straightened and turned his hands up, letting mine drop.

"But her family?"

"Already on their way to claim her remains. I'll speak with them, of course, find out more about her psychological health, but there is really not much more we can do." He grimaced and leaned toward me again, pressing his lips to my forehead. I felt them move against me as he said softly, "Let it go, Henna. We've done what we could, and sometimes that is enough."

How lovely he was, in all his flesh and blood. Heat seeped through me, and we both caught our breath at the flare that leaped between us. When he drew back, the room grew colder, and I wrapped my arms around myself, thinking of that woman in the woods all alone, stumbling from her car, lost in the dark. "But shouldn't we try to figure out why she thought that letter was so important?" I persisted.

Fletcher sighed and stepped around his desk. "I'll call you tonight," he said as the bulky black radio on his desk began to hiss and squawk. In the outer room, the dispatcher pressed a stale chocolate heart on me, patting my shoulder with her doughy hand. The wrapper was faded red tinfoil; inside, the heart was scaled white, old and crumbling, sweet on my tongue.

❄

When I got home, I dumped the doctor's bag on the chair next to the front door and rummaged through it, shifting my wallet, passport, receipts from the truck stop donut shop, the scraps of letter, a crumbling sheet of paper I couldn't place until I spotted the words *grown too old to tramp the fields* and remembered the *Snow Almanack*—faded scent of skunk and honeysuckle—and finally the small cream card at the very bottom of the bag, thick as a promise, unbent.

According to the Internet, the Extinction Museum was housed on a decommissioned aircraft carrier that had done a brief stint as a refugee camp before being auctioned off to the public. The website for the museum was grandiose, the language as colorful as Mr. Plover's attire. Filigreed script claimed *The World's Fair of the Future*, but you had to click through pages of art deco gates and baroque wooden doors and, finally, through a striped tent flap to get to any solid information. Apparently, Plover had amassed an eclectic collection of taxidermied and fossilized specimens of extinct animals and plants and other eccentricities, from a pair of intact mastodon tusks to an apex predator Orthacanthus shark preserved in shale to a bog body from the Bronze Age, burnished face captured in a rictus of despair. An embalmed blue whale was rigged to the side of the ship where it drifted realistically, its scarred flukes waving. A stainless-steel casket held a vial of freeze-dried smallpox virus. There were hearts and brains and livers of various disaster victims floating in formaldehyde, hundreds of birds, stuffed and posed in lifelike manner, a library of wax cylinder recordings of famous long-dead poets.

I scrolled through the gallery, amazed by the scope. The graphics were high resolution, the furnishings of the museum staunchly Victorian, glimpses of red velvet settees and intricately carved marble mantels, no hint of the warship beneath. Funereal sconces threw off a semblance of gaslight and the captions for the exhibits flickered on my computer screen.

In many of the photos, a woman appeared next to the item, for scale. Her hair was blond and ringletted, her buxom figure clad in a short gold-sequined dress. It wasn't until I peered more closely at the photos that I noticed there was not one woman but several, all styled identically, all with the same practiced smile. The museum traveled from port to port, a carnival of disappearance, with Plover as its ringmaster.

My printer growled and clattered as it churned out the downloaded pages. I could barely stand to take the time to fold them into my coat pocket before dashing out the door to Mariel's, Rembrandt loping in front of me into the snowy dusk.

❄

In the darkening evening, Mariel's house glowed like a lantern. I pressed the doorbell and waited a bit, then turned the knob. Unlocked, trusting soul. Mariel stood in the doorway to the kitchen, drying her hands on her apron. She gestured for me to join her, and I walked into the warmth and smell of frying. There was a platter of zucchini blossoms, delicately battered, in the center of the small square table. Where she found the flowers in this weather, I couldn't guess. Two plates waited, as if I had been expected.

She wouldn't let me talk while we ate. A cello concerto streamed from the speaker on the counter. The deep notes vibrated through the wood floors, the cabinets, up the lathed legs of the table. Mariel's left pinkie beat the time. She filled old honey jars with home-brewed cider, sharply spiced.

After we washed the dishes, I spread the printouts on the table and told her about Plover. The blue paper made the photos look as if the museum floated underwater. Mariel grimaced and pushed the sheets into a pile, flipped them over facedown. *Hubris,* she wrote on a notecard. And then, *Why is he here?* We mulled this over, each of us offering more fantastic suggestions. Maybe some indigenous breed of upstate lake fish was about to die out. Maybe there was a cache of recently discovered fossils under the snow, a Paleolithic man buried beneath the drugstore.

We turned from Plover to the dead woman, both of us eyeing the kitchen window, through which, over the ravine where the woman's car presumably lay, we could see the pinprick lights of the Vanderkey house where Plover was staying. Was there some connection between these two strangers to the village? I told Mariel about the letter, about how I'd determined it was from Lady Jane Franklin, and about Fletcher's information on the dead woman's doctoral studies. I took her through that ill-fated expedition, the facts spilling from me in a perfect recitation. Mariel drank globe after globe of cider and watched my mouth like a lover. I'd always had a good memory. Claire had been the one who could forget the little slights, the peculiar humiliations of youth, the fishhook rips of people's day-to-day cruelty. Claire always took the long view, like those old explorers, locked in the ice.

❄

On May 19, 1845, HMS *Terror* and HMS *Erebus* had set off into the cold seas with their fifty-nine-year-old captain—survivor of an overland Arctic expedition thirty years previously, fat with old age and prosperity, tarnished by a difficult governorship in Van Diemen's Land, bound tightly into his uniform, his heart constant as the new steam engines fitted into the ships. They carried thousands of tins of food to last them three years, barrels of lime juice and rum, twelve hundred books, a hand organ programmed with fifty different tunes, reams of writing paper, slates and chalk, two cases of art supplies, three hundred bars of soap, and a pet monkey. On board were one hundred twenty-nine souls encased in fragile flesh that must be fed and washed and tended to, sewn up and scraped bare and amused by various means. The last time anyone saw them was that same year, when a whaling ship made contact with them in Baffin Bay and wished them good journey as they entered the ice and disappeared.

After three years of silence, the British Admiralty started sending in ships. Lady Jane continually petitioned them to send more men and exerted pressure on American shippers to join the search as well. No one found any trace of the Franklin expedition. Rumors abounded. The Inuit told stories of men crossing the ice, of massacres and abandoned sledges, and produced brass buttons as evidence. Bottles on Russian shores were collected and sent to London in hopes they'd come from the lost ships, but they turned out to be Norwegian fishing floats. Tundra voles wheeked at each other as dark shapes staggered over the field of white. The *Erebus* and *Terror* never sailed back out of the polar fog.

In 1851, a group including Elisha Kent Kane—that dashing doctor, engaged to a fraudulent spiritualist, health wrecked by the Arctic, fated to die young just a few years later—found evidence that Franklin had wintered over on Beechey Island. Three graves dated 1846 were found alongside piles of six hundred empty food tins, each weighted with a basalt pebble, veined with quartz. A pair of cashmere gloves was found, also each anchored by a pebble, as if laid out to dry.

My heart rapped against my sternum as I relayed these details. The stones could be laid out in a line, the veins connecting, but no map could be derived from them. The cairns meant to hold messages and records stood empty, as if the men had already given up thoughts of the world below.

❄

The spell broke. Mariel snored quietly, her head thrown back against the kitchen chair, her hand curled around a capped pen. I gathered up the printouts from the Extinction Museum, roused Rembrandt, and dove into the cold night. The snow had stopped, but my footsteps from earlier were half-filled. I went slowly. Rembrandt must have been tired, because he stayed with me for once, stepping behind me in my tracks.

Ahead of me, I could see the dark shape of my house clearly. And then, between me and its silhouette, a small flicker like a cigarette lighter or the glimpse of a flashlight being doused. I stopped, and Rembrandt peered around me, growling. Then he was off, barking wildly as he sprinted toward the house. I followed more gradually because I'd already guessed who it was. By the time I'd gotten to the door, Fletcher was tossing away his cigarette and twisting the knob to gesture me in, Rembrandt slinking through his feet. Fletcher caught me as I stepped around him, pulling me into his arms.

"You have to learn to lock up, Henna." He released me as quickly as he had grabbed me, and I dropped the papers I was carrying. They spread round us on the snowy walk in a puddle of blue. Fletcher was faster than me, and he clicked his lighter again to glance at the sheets. I saw the flash of teeth. His voice was strained when he said, "So, you've met Plover."

"You know him?" I took the papers from him and stepped into the light of the open doorway.

"I know everyone in town," he said, forcing a grin. "Especially the strange ones." He tapped me on the chin and reached past me for the doorknob, nudging me inside as he started to pull the door shut.

"You don't want to come in?" I struck a pretty good seductress pose, despite the snow melting off me—the kind Claire and I had practiced in the mirror hundreds of times before we'd go cross-eyed and snaggle-toothed and fall into guffaws at our jutting hips and breasts.

"I have to get going," he murmured, leaning in for a kiss. Wisp of steel and caramel. "I just wanted to be sure you made it home safely."

I wondered how he'd known I'd gone out. And how he'd known the front door was unlocked. Presumably this was what it was like, dating the police chief.

I looked for his truck. My drive was empty, as was the street. As if reading my mind, Fletcher gestured to a pair of cross-country skis propped in the shadow of the house. "Good exercise," he said. "Lock the door, Henna."

MAGNETIC POLE

ACH MORNING, HER NIECE SOPHY laid out her stationery and inkwell and blotting sheets. The desktop was scarred over from heavy use. Jane signed her letters to the papers "Impartiality." She wrote a hundred letters a week, mostly to those who might be convinced to help send ships to look for her husband. She established subscriptions, bought two ships of her own, flirted, coerced. She summoned men to her. In her modest parlor, a portrait of her husband peering over her shoulder, desiccated reindeer tongues in a jar on the pianoforte, she entertained Dickens, Tennyson, admirals and geographers, politicians and industrialists. She had great hopes for America, where money ripened like plums. The American businessmen loved her, sent ship after ship into the ice for her, and it was just happy chance that they made a profit along the way. Her husband had been transformed into a set of coordinates that everyone wanted to discover. She had imagined him such ever since their first meeting, a speck with such pull, a spark she could bring blazing into light.

CHAPTER NINE

I CLOSED THE DOOR BEHIND me but did not lock it. I'd always hated being told what to do. Maybe it was natural perversity. Maybe it was part of being a twin. When you were a twin, you lived a tale of misplaced lovers and secret passages. Everyone always hoped they were being tricked. Everyone always was. In the forest, we built altars. We gathered berries, sweet and deadly. In rundown bars, we glowed. We never dressed the same, but no one could tell us apart. We were supposed to follow the same path, eat the same foods, be separated at birth and discovered through fateful mishap in old age. One of us was supposed to have stolen the seal skin given to my father long ago and ripped herself away from this life. Maybe one of us had.

I threw a handful of dog treats at Rembrandt, and he settled down with a snort. My recitation at Mariel's had made me curious about the exact timeline of the discoveries around Franklin's expedition. My bag still stood by the door, and I thought for a moment about Fletcher and his certainty that I wasn't home and my house was unlocked. Everything was a jumble inside the bag. It would have been hard to tell if anything had been touched. The scraps of letter were still there, and the page from the snow almanac. I felt a pang of guilt. Not only had I withheld the fragments of letter from Fletcher, I'd stolen from his grandfather's archive. It would serve me right if he had snooped and discovered it. Perhaps that was why he was in such a hurry to get away.

I dug out my notes from earlier in the day and went to the sun-room, where I kept a stack of books for reference. There was a thick one bound in maroon linen titled simply *Arctic Exploration* that was chock full of dates and maps. I skimmed over the story of Elisha Kent Kane on Beechey Island in 1851. No more evidence of the fates of the men of the *Terror* and the *Erebus* was discovered until 1854, a year before the date on the scrap of letter, nine years after Franklin had gone missing. That same year, the Admiralty had taken the names of Franklin and his crew off their books, essentially pronouncing them dead. John Rae returned with tales he had heard from the Inuit, stories of scores of bodies of white men strewn across King William Island. The dead bodies made a trail that led nowhere, white into more white, ice unending.

Rae relayed the Inuit's observations of saw marks on the bodies, the human remains found in the cooking pots. He brought back a royal badge Sir John Franklin had always worn around his neck that the Inuit said they found by the pots and bones. England was shocked and sickened. They could scarcely believe that the arrows of their nation could have engaged in that "last dread alternative," despite hints of such behavior on previous expeditions, including Franklin's earlier trek, during which he was forced to kill a man who persisted in bringing back suspicious caribou meat from jaunts on which his companions died in accidents.

Lady Jane was particularly determined in her denial, and wrote letters to the papers and to friends disputing Rae's account until her hand and arm seized up and she took to bed. Her niece fed her warm broth as they plotted a trip round the world to escape the gamey stench of London.

❄

Rembrandt tugged at my sleeve, and I got up to let him out. When I opened the door, the cold was a slap. Snow was drifting down again. Winter without end. All of us for miles around, frozen into our houses, reading the same news, shoring up our stocks of bottled water and gasoline, dehydrated food and ammunition, listening to the earth crack.

❄

I rested my head on my hand, flipping through the notes, trying to estimate how many days of hunger it took to break a person, trying to imagine the dead men, lying huddled on the ice where they had fallen, their living compatriots too weak to bury them, the temptation of so much wasted meat.

And then, redemption, for Lady Jane at least. In 1857, she bought another ship, the *Fox*, wily, determined, with sharp teeth. Francis Leopold McClintock captained it, and two years later, after being trapped in the ice pack two winters, he found a cairn on King William Island circled by abandoned clothing and rope, cooking utensils, books and medical supplies, as if the men had been constructing a target to alert future explorers. The cairn held a sheet of paper with coordinates written out ten years before by one of *Erebus*'s officers, and round the margins of this note, written in another hand, signed by the second-in-command, was the record of being beset two winters and a summer until the crew had resolved to leave the ships and trek overland the following day. And finally, scrawled in tiny letters at the edge of the page, news of the death of Sir John Franklin months before, in June of 1847, well before any desperate measures would have been taken.

Lady Jane seized upon this news of her husband, now cleared of any taint of cannibalism, with joy and relief. Proof of her husband's death, after so many years of waiting, became a celebration, a grand dinner in honor of McClintock's voyage. There were aspics and cream cakes, French wines and molded ice. For the men of the *Fox*, Lady Jane brought a clutch of pocket watches, all still as stones, unwound in their leather cases. She gifted the captain with a silver model of his ship, heavy as an anchor, impermeable as her own conviction in her husband's noble heart.

❄

Outside it was clear, and still it snowed. I called for Rembrandt, and his warm body shot past me into the house. The stars were spear points puncturing the night, the moon a scythe swinging free to the south. The snow fell in handfuls, powdery—the husks of dead stars, water that traveled by sky. I felt with my blood, and their diffuse vibrations shivered through me. The murmur of low voices, ghost sailors dragging their wooden boats over the ice, one man singing something I couldn't catch. A child's song perhaps, filled with knives and birds, a song for dreaming.

❄

My father's studio was always a mess, a hodgepodge of tortured paint tubes and mossy drop cloths. He liked to paint naked women and dead things. He always made them beautiful. In the dream, a line of small weasel skulls stared at me from the long shelf on the wall. Behind me was a bank of windows, shuddering in the wind coming off the ocean. A storm was building, and even inside, the air was thick with ozone. My sister was there, shaking my shoulder. "Henna, wake up," she said, and her breath was tinged with violets and dirt. Then the walls shattered and the sea came in.

❄

I woke to the smell of turpentine and Rembrandt standing on my chest, licking my face frantically. I couldn't breathe. I shoved him off, only to find my bedroom full of smoke, my lungs drowning in the viscous black fumes. There was a roaring somewhere—downstairs, it seemed—and an insidious crackling closer.

Pulling the neck of my T-shirt over my mouth and nose, I dragged Rembrandt to the window and shoved at the ancient wooden sash. The window screamed in its cage. My sight was getting dimmer, narrowing down to a snowflake aperture as I pounded against the aluminum screen. When it finally popped from its frame, I heaved Rembrandt's great weight onto the sill and pushed him out, not daring to watch how he landed. For a moment, I hesitated, looking around the room for something I might take with me to charm my descent. Cartoon visions of sheets turning to parachutes flitted through my smoke-addled head, but then the groaning of the house took up a new tenor and I heard glass shattering. So I cast myself out the window, violently scraping my hips as I shimmied through into thin air.

The fall was a chill few seconds, and then I plummeted into a snow bank next to Rembrandt. It was like slamming into the ocean while surfing, and for a couple of minutes, I allowed myself to tumble down into the cold and dark, everything muffled except the cadence of my breath returning. A furnace lighting, a shell singing, the wet hum of the lungs performing their bloody task. I could have stayed there forever, in love with my own inhalations and exhalations, the cold air sharp as a blade in my throat. Instead, I scrambled blindly toward the forest, pulling a protesting Rembrandt, until my muscles gave out and I turned to watch the house burn.

It looked perfectly normal, except for the aura of smoke pouring from its edges. The only part visibly on fire was my glassed-in writing studio, which was a blossom of flame. The room writhed with light, and I imagined the keys of the typewriter jumping in the heat, as if a ghost touched them. Then the windows gave way, and shards of glass pelted me like sleet from the impassive sky.

❄

Fire trucks arrived like a scourge of banshees. More entertainment for the endless winter. Rembrandt buried his nose in the snow as I ran my hands gently over him, searching for cuts or broken bones. I lay my head on his flank, too tired to make myself known to the rapidly multiplying rescuers, half expecting the red-eared police officer to gambol around the corner of the house any minute, eyes alight at this new drama.

It was Fletcher who found me, of course. His boots appeared before me, and I marveled at their high gloss in this inhospitable terrain. Then his strong hands grasped my scored forearms to raise me to a sitting position. The cuts from the flying glass stung, and I shrank away. Behind him, a searchlight flicked on and voices cried out in relief.

He was in shadow, a dark form leaning toward me, saying, "Henna, I never…" when the paramedics appeared with their orange cases and swinging flashlights. They unfurled a stretcher as if summoning it from the snow and started encasing me in plastic and blankets. Fletcher cupped my cheeks and leaned in to place a chaste kiss on my hair. My bloodied hips were screaming. Cellophane packets were being ripped open at a startling rate, and I felt a needle prick my inner elbow. My vision was narrowing down again, the snow falling harder around us. I thought I heard Mariel's seal-bark laugh.

Someone called for the police chief, and Fletcher stepped back, releasing me. His hands came away from my face black.

❄

They took me to the hospital in the next town over. I remember nothing about the ambulance ride except the conviction that they were trying to smother me with the oxygen mask. I pulled it off over and over until they strapped my wrists to the gurney, and then I was diving down again, the plastic bubble sucked tight to my skin by the weight of the ocean.

❄

In the hospital, I was the lucky one, as always. Nothing could kill me, it seemed. I coughed up gobs of dark mucus, my throat raw. Mariel came to visit and we just stared at each other, neither one of us inclined to talk. She was keeping Rembrandt for me; maybe the dog, unfazed by his forced evacuation, had chewed up all her pens. She handed me a twist of silver paper before she left. Inside was a bit of honeycomb, dried up, a miracle of compartmentalization, tough to chew, redolent of unimaginable summer. I amused myself by making the water in the IV bag slosh. Someone had stuck small Band-Aids over the cuts on my arms—thirty-two of them. They were the kind made for kids, patterned with brightly colored animals with abnormally large eyes.

When Fletcher entered the room holding a huge arrangement of yellow spider mums and day lilies, I could have screamed in relief. Finally, someone with the power to get me out of there.

"I am so sorry, Henna," he said. I tried to say something to convince him to unhook me and take me from this muffled space, but my throat closed up around the words. "You know the house had no smoke alarms?" he asked reprovingly, leaning toward me to pick up a lock of my hair. He took my chin in his hand and turned my face from side to side, inspecting for damage. "You could have been killed," he said and released me. "It may not have been an accident."

For some reason, this had not occurred to me before now. Then I remembered the smell of turpentine from my dream, the way the fire had been concentrated in the sun porch where my notes were. The room started to quiver. The water in the IV bag, the half-full pink plastic pitcher, the vase of flowers all began to bubble furiously. The pipes in the bathroom squealed as the taps burst open. I pulled the IV out of my arm and shot out of bed, startling Fletcher so that he rocked backward on the chair and nearly toppled over. All of my muscles protested, but I moved determinedly across the room toward the door.

Fletcher grabbed my hip, awakening a flare of pain there. "Henna, sit down," he said, forcing me back to the edge of the bed. "Where are you going? Your house is a wreck, and all of your things are smoke-damaged and waterlogged. It will take weeks to sort things out."

"I'll go to a hotel," I said, except of course there were no hotels. "A bed and breakfast," I amended. There was one in town, Verbena Manor, a tumbling-down Victorian crusted with gingerbread and layers of yellow paint. It was owned by a wild-eyed septuagenarian who reportedly mowed his lawn in the middle of the night all summer with no regard for his sleeping guests.

"With crazy old Evan?" Fletcher took my hands in his. "Don't you have a friend you could go to?"

I thought of Mariel, but if someone was trying to hurt me, I didn't want to drag her into it. A few days with Rembrandt was enough of a cross for her to bear. The silence stretched out.

"Well, that settles it," he said. "You'll stay with me. My house is certainly large enough."

I drew back a bit, slipping my hands out of his. The animal eyes up and down my arms stared at him.

"Don't worry," he said with a wry smile. "You'll have a chaperone. My mother still lives there." He stood up briskly, slapping his palms against his thighs. It was settled; I felt it like a tide drawing against me. My throat hurt too much to protest.

POLE OF INACCESSIBILITY

*H*E TRIED TO CONTACT HER in their second wintering over. The ships were locked tight. The ice pack heaved and clutched. They were seeds caught fast. At night he sent out his thoughts. He dreamed a ghost girl in Liverpool and made her memorize his location. Other ghosts gathered round. The ghosts of his crew that had died from bad food or fever or boredom were of no use to him. They were trapped too. He had to go farther afield.

The child ghosts were the most intrepid. They came equipped with sextants and stubs of lead, picked up in their travels. They liked the names of his ships and rubbed the ice away from the painted script. The first year, he wrote her letters as well, but gave up when they filled his drawer. He knew his duty was to keep good records. His knuckles didn't want to cooperate, so he had to conserve his writing for striking measurements and dates in the unwieldy log book.

Sleep was where his mind could travel. The ghost children drew him forward by his cuffs until he could almost see her, perched in the drawing room, head bent over her correspondence. The concept of a drawing room amazed him—a miracle of curtained windows that opened onto earth and grass and cobbled streets. His throat clenched with desire, but no matter how hard he tried to say her name, she never looked up, just kept writing, a fine reproach.

CHAPTER TEN

ONCE THE DOCTOR HAD GIVEN her consent to my release, Mariel came to get me. I hugged her when she handed over the three-pack of cotton underwear. She also gave me one of her white sweaters and a pair of loose linen pants, also white, with a blue drawstring at the waist. Whereas Mariel always looked so elegant in her monochromatic wardrobe, I looked like I was still in hospital attire, recently escaped, needle-marked and consommé-fatigued.

She dropped me off at my battered house. The walls were streaked black, and furniture was scattered in the front yard where the firefighters had dragged it to be sure no sparks remained. The flaxen couch looked like a dying beast, skin splotchy and torn, heaved onto a drift of snow. The mattress was a perfect study in despair, as all bare mattresses are. It was as if my liver were on display for all the neighbors. Bookshelves and cabinets were a heap of broken wood. Inside, things weren't so bad except for the smell of charred plaster and burnt wire. My doctor's bag still sat by the door, slightly damp but intact.

I wasn't supposed to go into the sunroom, nor upstairs, since the extent of the structural damage was still unclear. There were sooty footprints across all the floorboards, and I reminded myself to order something to be delivered to the various volunteer fire stations in the area, maybe coffee cakes or giant muffins, breakfast food, emblematic of rebirth. I snuck up to my bedroom anyway, staying close to the wall. It looked nearly untouched except for the missing mattress and the sound of dripping.

It seemed there should be something precious here, something to save. But I had left all sentimental possessions behind when I moved. The paintings and letters and books were packed into a barn at the edge of the Pacific. All safe, boarded up, a musty heart with eaves and a rusted winch. In that barn, there was a velvet smock of my mother's, patterned green-orange, bare in sections. Claire and I used to tease that she was molting. My father's hardened half-used tubes of paint crept there like snails through the dark and dust. Stacks and stacks of portraits of my parents floated in the haymow, all scarred with a small red C.

❄

In my chill, smoke-damaged room, nothing was salvageable; it all lay in sodden piles that were easy to abandon. So I gathered up Rembrandt and ignored Mariel's offers of a place to stay or at least a change of clothes to replace the ones streaked now with ash and mud. I went to Fletcher's house empty-handed, except for my battered old bag, so acrid with smoke that I resolved to leave it in the car. I was a bride with no dowry, and Rembrandt sighed happily at how weightless we were as we sped along, his affection narrowed down to the nasty sucking bone I'd picked up at the grocery store when I'd stopped for dog food.

The drive that led to Fletcher's home was a ribbon of wet black between two proud rows of pines. The snowy branches were flocked wings against the blue sky. He had implied the fire was no accident, but hadn't speculated on who would have set it. Presumably, the same person who had rummaged through my kitchen and who had locked me in the tower room. The same person who had driven that woman to her death. But why? What about the letter was so dangerous that someone would kill over it?

My list of suspects was meager. It was a relatively unpopulated area and I had been somewhat reclusive. Fletcher, himself, was a likely prospect, but I couldn't figure out why he'd have harmed the woman. He'd also had ample opportunities to menace me at close range and hadn't. I tried to ignore the fact that the frisson of pleasure between us whenever we touched might be clouding my judgment.

What other suspects were there? Harris, feeling possessive of his Arctic collection, threatened somehow by the appearance of the dead woman? Plover with his weird joviality about the death of species came to mind, but I couldn't figure out any connection between him and the letter. Still, there was something odd in how Plover's expansive personality clashed with his reclusive behavior, and how I hadn't seen hide nor hair of him until I started finding pieces of the letter.

It was possible that it had all been an accident. The woman had simply wandered astray. The person in my kitchen, imagined. The tower room, a prank. My house was old and riddled with bad wiring.

Rembrandt huffed dismissively in the backseat. A dog with a bone, I thought as I drove through the arcade of pines, and the song came back—the sailor ditty sung by men hungry for marrow, for flesh, for anything not canned or dried. Men who had sailed, eyes open, toward probable disaster, all for the lure of discovery. My blood settled then for the first time since the fire, stubborn and full in my veins, as if I was stepping into a pool of still water, hidden but close, near enough to feel its gravity.

❄

Fletcher's house was enormous and dingy white, Italianate, with red brick chimneys sprouting from it. Twelve large gleaming windows, flanked by peeling green shutters, stared onto the drive. The front door was hidden under a portico and a swath of brown vines. The ivy crept all over the façade, a blight that probably looked romantic in summer, but now resembled nothing more than withered veins, sucking sustenance out of the house. I shook my head as

I stopped the car in the circle drive. Even as I peered through the windshield at the looming edifice, all the curtains seemed to twitch at once, the same dark form flitting across each of the dozen windows. Rembrandt raised his head and barked, and I craned my neck further to see a great winged shape glide over us, an owl headed into the forest behind the house, beautiful and sudden as an indrawn breath.

❋

The owl was once believed to be a harbinger of shipwreck. And here I was, cast up on the shores of Fletcher's domain. Even though his house was technically still in the village, it was high up on the hill, the only house on the ridge, surrounded by the same woods that stretched into my backyard. The road to get here skirted the densely thicketed ravine. Presumably, the dead woman's car lay somewhere in that fissure, covered in groaning snow. Grandmother owl, sharp talons, all-seeing. I felt something watching me as I prodded Rembrandt from the car. He snarled around the edges of his sopping bone.

Fletcher appeared on the porch, almost as if he had leapt from the doorway. I trudged toward him, suddenly feeling every cut and scrape. My lungs worked against the unseasonably cold air. Fletcher waited for me and gave me a half hug, decorous and hospitable. He bent his head to my ear and there was a whisper of sound, my name, I thought, and then the fleeting touch of his lips on my neck. Before I could lean into him, he straightened briskly and gestured to the wide gap in the doorway where the threshold should be.

"Rot," he explained, and then, to my surprise, hoisted me up in his arms and gracefully stepped over the empty space, into the shadowy foyer of the house, which was barely warmer than the outside air.

I had just started to squirm when a woman's voice proclaimed, "Charming," and dark separated from dark, coalescing into the figure of a sturdy, well-groomed woman with highlighted hair cut in a trim bob and age lines dragging at her jaw.

Fletcher released me with a jarring thud. I clung tightly to Rembrandt. "Mother," he said, pushing me toward the woman.

She didn't move to extend her hand, just squinted at me and said, "What is that creature?" For a moment, I thought she was talking about me, intensely conscious of my stained baggy clothes, my singed hair, my bare face. She pursed perfectly outlined lips and brushed her palms nervously against her rose wool skirt. "Is it a dog?"

Rembrandt plodded over the missing threshold to the oriental rug and deposited the slimy bone on a stylized rose. Then he flopped onto his side, hoisted one leg, and assiduously began to clean himself.

Fletcher's mother's face twisted in disgust. "Dogs do not belong in this house. We keep birds," she announced.

"Oh, he won't bother them. He's far too lazy," I said. My comment fell flat as both Fletcher and his mother regarded me silently. I stepped forward and extended my hand. "I'm Henna. Thank you for inviting me to stay."

Fletcher's mother jerked back as if shocked, and then reached out to brush my hand with the tips of her fingers. "Oh yes," she said absently. "Your house burned. Well, you may call me Eleanor." She straightened the cuffs of her pale pink cashmere sweater. Raising her eyebrows at Fletcher, she said, "I thought we would put her up in the attic. It is perfectly comfortable up there now that we've installed radiators."

"No, Mother. Henna is not staying in the old servants' quarters." Fletcher sounded amused. "I asked Dita to prepare the blue room."

"But the rugs," Eleanor protested, eyeing Rembrandt.

"Mother, it will be fine. Now let's find Henna some clothes."

Eleanor turned her skeptical gaze on me. "She's slender enough. She'd fit into some of the Aunties' things."

"Of course," Fletcher said, taking me by the hand and pulling me toward the wide staircase that dominated the foyer. The banister was gleaming and sinuous, a fanciful swirl anchored by finials that had scales cut into the mahogany. A slate blue runner of thick carpet muffled our steps. The house smelled musty, as old houses tend to when closed up all winter. Rembrandt trudged after us, lump of bone dangling from his jowls.

Eleanor called out, "Franklin, don't forget the reverend and Valerie are coming for dinner. She will need something suitable for company."

My skin chilled at the sound of the name I'd been obsessing over the past week, and I stopped on the stairs, dragging Fletcher to a halt with me. "What did she call you?" I whispered.

"Later," he said, with that surfer smile that first drew me to him. He raised his eyebrows and lowered his voice to the pretend hiss of a villain in a melodrama. "First, we have to get you out of those horrible clothes."

Rembrandt snuffled impatiently and edged past us, proceeding up the endless staircase. Below us, I heard a sigh of disapproval and the clicking of heels moving away, perfectly controlled, the tick of a metronome, just as several grandfather clocks began to chime the hour in unison, filling the hall with the sound of breaking things.

❋

The bedroom was clad in intensely blue plaster and was bare of furniture except for a huge sleigh bed of dark wood and a matching armoire crested with a carved eagle. The windows were diamond-paned and did not open. Curtains and coverlet were navy velvet, and there was an armada of pillows in ruffled cerulean silk. Rembrandt gave one yelp and retired to the black space under the bed. Fletcher had departed to retrieve the Aunties' clothing. I imagined a box filled with twin sets and wool skirts.

I cracked the massive door and peered into the hallway. It was midafternoon and dark as midnight in the hall. Strange cries were floating up the stairway, and I wondered what kind of birds Eleanor kept.

A particularly loud shriek came from outside, and I went to the window that looked out over the gardens in the back. Fletcher was rounding the corner of the house with a woman slung over his shoulder. She was bundled in coat and scarf, but her long red hair trailed in the snow. The muffled sounds seemed like laughter. Then they disappeared into the house.

❋

I had yet to investigate the other door in the room, painted the same electric blue of the walls. It opened into a bathroom, and when I flipped the light switch, it took a minute for my eyes to adjust to the sudden brilliance. The bathroom was nearly as spacious as the bedroom. Dozens of ornate gold-framed mirrors were arranged like puzzle pieces, and the slivers of wall that showed between the frames were covered in crimson damask wallpaper. The effect was of a hundred wounds, bloody slashes interrupting the repetition of my shocked image. One corner was taken up by a vast sunken tub, tiled in large squares of red marble, almost a pool. The water, when I turned it on, gushed out of a gleaming trough-shaped faucet, bounteous as any mountain cascade. There was no soap, but on the counter beside the enormous shell-shaped sink was a thick pile of burgundy towels.

The tub filled rapidly, the water reflecting the tiles in a disturbingly gory manner. But the heat and steam as I stepped into the bath were pure bliss after the perfunctory wipe-downs the nurses had performed in the hospital. I sank down and leaned back against the tile ledge.

The ceiling was painted with a scene of nymphs or muses, some buxom breed of naked females whose profession was cavorting. Parts of the panorama were quite detailed, and I was so engrossed by the attention lavished on various anatomical impossibilities that I didn't immediately realize that all of the ladies wore gloves, some opera length, some buttoned, some mere wristlets. All in blushing pink, just a few shades darker than their skin. When I noticed, it startled me so much that I laughed, the first big, full laugh I'd had in several days. My throat was still recovering from this exertion when the knock came at the bathroom door.

I rose quickly in an attempt to get to the towels and called out something garbled, but was still in the tub when the door swung open and Fletcher and the woman with the red hair walked in. They both stood transfixed for a moment. The three of us were reflected many times over, my bruised body mottled like a chameleon's skin.

"Dita, a towel," Fletcher snapped, raising his gaze decorously to the ceiling. I had a moment of compunction for his gentlemanly distress, but what could they have expected, barging into the bathroom like that? Dita gave me one of those amused looks that beautiful women give the rest of us and stepped languidly toward the sink. In the mirrors, her red hair flashed, the same shade as the wallpaper. She was a clot moving in the veins.

"Here," she said, proffering the towel. It was so big, it wrapped around me twice and dragged in the water. "You've stolen my entrance," she said, giving me an assessing look. "Dita, short for Aphrodite, at your service."

"Dita is our housekeeper," Fletcher explained, finally looking at me again. He reached out a hand and helped haul me out of the deep tub. I stood dripping onto the cold floor. Dita linked arms with Fletcher and laughed.

"We brought you the clothes, and it gave Fletcher quite a start to see you'd gone missing." Goosebumps rose on my arms. "Be careful, Henna. No more accidents, okay?" she said, as if we were old friends. "Come on." She pulled at Fletcher. "Let her try on the antiques."

Again, her laughter rang out, and Fletcher smiled in response. He brushed his fingertips over my wet shoulder, and they left, the door snicking shut behind them. I had to step back into the bath to reach the drain plug. The water, so soothing before, had chilled.

NORTHWEST PASSAGE

LACK SILK, BLACK LACE, BLACK feathers, black poplin. Black gloves for day, black gloves for evening. Black wool, black boots, black slippers, black short veil, black long veil, black straw hats for summer, black fur muff for when her hands grew chilled. Black stockings and underthings. It stained, left a tinge of gray. Jane put on mourning a few years after her husband went missing, not in acknowledgement of his death, but rather of her loss. She played the false widow, the inverse bride, waiting for her lover to return. Without the weeds, would anyone remember she was married? The black bled out of her in lines on the map, new locations inscribed in ink that had to be warmed next to the skin before it could be used. But when the Admiralty gave up on Captain Franklin and took his name off the active roster, rendering him and his men deceased, Jane switched to the brightest pink and green attire. Her husband was not dead and never would be so long as he was missing. Missing, he and his men eternally completed their journey, recorded great feats, bridged continents, rested sparingly, waited to be uncovered.

CHAPTER ELEVEN

*I*N THE MIDDLE OF THE bare room sat a blond trunk, camel-backed, bound with tarnished metal strips. I popped the latches with some effort and lifted the heavy lid. The smell of cedar and clementine wafted out. There was a layer of yellowed tissue paper, then a froth of lavender. I held up a silk chemise and matching drawers, edged in deep violet lace. Beneath this, another set, aqua with teal trim. More tissue paper, rustling like moth wings, and a corset with fraying twill laces, hand-hammered eyelets running up the edges. Five pairs of silk stockings, cocooned in square white envelopes, the kind used for invitations. Then four shirts of cotton lawn, two dove gray, two hyacinth blue. A long black serge skirt and matching jacket with slightly puffed shoulders. The same items in tweedy brown. Kid-leather ankle boots, also black, worn a little at the toe, a button hook. The Aunties were proving to be a surprise.

Crushed beneath the other things, there was a long chiffon gown in midnight blue. I shook it out, and the smell of citrus grew stronger. A few beads clattered to the floor from the intricately worked bodice. Pinned at the shoulder was a bunch of some small withered flower, maybe orange blossoms. The pleated skirt trembled and settled

With some trepidation, I held it to my chest and stepped back into the bathroom. In the mirrors, my eyes shone silver, my skin waxy as a pearl.

❊

The clothes fit perfectly. It took a long time to get dressed for dinner. Rembrandt slept through my transformation. I had to wear the corset with the blue dress to fasten the buttons running down the side. The corset was front-lacing and it formed a carapace, molded by some other woman, still holding her shape. I was doubled again then, my body twinning her curves, malleable enough. In a drawer in the bathroom, I found a welcome cache of toiletries that looked like they dated from the 1950s. A tortoiseshell comb and a Bakelite toothbrush were stacked next to a small tin of baking powder and a rose-shaped soap wrapped in crumbling paper. Best of all was a packet of hairpins, ancient and sharp as needles.

With much twisting and piling and a few minor scalp wounds, I managed to get my hair up off my neck and out of my face. It took a few minutes to figure out the boots, and by the time I had them on, my abdomen was aching from the corset cutting into it. Claire would have laughed to see me playing dress-up. Dark blue butterfly shaking out damp wings.

Last, I unfastened the dead flowers from the dress and pinned them to the lining of the trunk, a talisman against decay. The blackened pin slid into the pad of my index finger as I secured the bouquet. The drop of blood that welled up was straight out of a fairy tale, round and fat, velvet red.

❈

I had a plan, of course—I, who had grown into a life of research like a nautilus into its shell. It seemed possible that Fletcher or someone in his household knew more about the woman's death than they were letting on. As when I'd visited the hawthorn bush the morning after finding the woman, I felt the impulse to put myself in her place, to follow where she had gone. Had she been to this decaying house?

In the hospital, there had been a map of the area next to the nurses' station. It was sixty years old, so a bit hard to interpret, but on my mandatory constitutionals I'd scanned the topography, marked the distance between Fletcher's house and the rise where my own house perched, eyed the dips and creases of the woods between. It was plausible that the woman's trajectory could be traced back to here. Perhaps there were signs of her I could glean somehow. My lack of anywhere else to turn for shelter seemed almost fortuitous.

And of course there was the charge between me and Fletcher, the way his presence was pulling my dowsing back to the surface, the sting I felt in the air when he was near. My plan was to go everywhere I was forbidden and see what else might arise at my touch. My plan was to push hard against any soft spots, press until they oozed.

❄

After giving Rembrandt a bowl of dog food, which I'd smuggled upstairs, I followed the sound of voices to a sitting room on the main floor. Fletcher was standing with his back to me, talking to an older man I'd never met—the reverend, presumably. Eleanor had her head bent over a book held by another woman. Both of them wore sheath dresses and low-heeled pumps. The reverend's wife was clad in beige, maybe flax, but Fletcher's mother's dress was a marvel of green silk, splashed with yellow and orange tropical flowers. Her shoes were gray snakeskin.

Dita was the first to see me, since she was sprawled on the toile-covered couch that faced the door. "Ah," she exclaimed. "A blast from the past."

Fletcher turned and hurried across the room to me, looking as he had on our one date in his sports coat, with his cowlicks tamped down. "Lovely," he said, taking my hand and stepping back in appreciation, laughter and something warmer in his eyes. Again, I considered the ramifications of staying in the same house as him, of having him so close at hand. Against the corset, my skin flushed.

Eleanor looked up from the book. "The Aunties always did have good taste," she said. "It's a pity your father gave away most of their clothes to that upstart historical society."

Fletcher put his palm at the small of my back. "This is Reverend Hazelton and his wife, Val."

"Jim," the reverend said, coming forward to shake my hand. He was a tall man, almost gaunt, and had a mop of unruly gray hair and thick tinted glasses.

His wife smiled at me and said, "What a wonderful dress. It fits you perfectly."

Dita stood up briskly, the gold caftan she wore settling around her bare feet. "Now that we are all here, let's start dinner before it is inedible," she said, shooing us out of the room. As we left, I noticed a cluster of bird cages in the far corner of the room, shrouded in black cloth.

❄

The dining room was dimly lit by several oil lamps positioned on the shelves and on the long table that had been pushed up against the windows. In the center of the room was a low round coffee table, obviously carried in from elsewhere in the house. Sofa cushions and pillows surrounded the table and an orange-glazed tagine sat in the middle of it. The smells of cumin and roasted onion overlay the scent of damp that seemed to permeate the house.

Dita clapped her hands and started assigning us cushions. I sat between Fletcher and Val and watched as Eleanor lowered herself gamely to the ground on the other side of her son. "Dita's whims," she grumbled, but she smiled indulgently at the girl and folded her hands decorously in her lap. Dita lifted the top of the tagine to reveal golden chicken mounded with lemon slices and green olives. She disappeared into what must have been the kitchen and returned with a large bowl of couscous and a platter of flatbread. Small dishes of fiery red paste sat at each place. Everything was perfectly cooked, redolent of marjoram and saffron, the faint tinge of the lamp oil.

Val was the one to bring up the dead woman. "Any news?" she said across the table to Fletcher. He summarized what he had already told me, said they were searching for her car, that the abnormally heavy snowfall was slowing their efforts. A weight seemed to lift from the group when Fletcher told us her parents had already come and gone, taking the remains with them.

"That road is a menace," Val said. "I don't dare open my eyes when Jim drives us up here in the winter."

Eleanor spoke slowly, as if the wine or the heat of the harissa thickened her tongue. "The ravine has always been our very own moat. It keeps what it claims." She giggled, a strange sound coming from her. Fletcher put the back of his hand to her cheek, as if checking for fever.

"Mother," he said. "Things change." Eleanor flashed him a glare, but reached up to clasp his hand, drawing it back down to the table.

The reverend broke the silence with a stream of stories about parish politics and the fundraising efforts to build a gazebo on the village green. "How many gazebos do we need?" teased Dita.

"Bonneport has three," Eleanor replied, her brusque tone restored, and she and Val launched into strategizing over sponsorships from nearby businesses and tag sales, periodically interrupted by the others' joking suggestions. The reverend had heard about some enterprising people the next county over who were filling up their pickups with snow and driving it as fast as they could down to the warm states, selling it by the ounce on the roadside.

Dessert was baklava, dripping with honey. "Local," Dita said as she sliced the pastry's many skins with a long silver knife. I thought of

Mariel's bees tight in their hives. Fletcher passed around tiny glasses of sweet wine. We grew quiet as we sipped, and the flames sputtered in their tall hurricane shades. We stayed there until the wine was gone, the chicken turned to bone and scrap, and March died into April, a cacophony of chimes that broke our trance.

When I rose, I stumbled, legs asleep after the long dinner, and there was the sound of tearing silk. Eleanor gasped and Fletcher took her arm, swiftly steering her out of the room. Dita walked the reverend and his wife to the front door, where I could hear them murmuring about the cold. I looked down to see a large rip in the seam over my hip. My calves and ankles tingled with a thousand snowflakes as the blood rushed home.

Home. I felt a pang of longing for my shuttered childhood house, the blowing sand, the seaweed with its bulbous tips strewn across the porch steps, the gulls crying in the sunset. And here I was, surrounded by antiques made of long-gone tree species, damask wallpaper, crown molding, the weight of years of accumulating and shucking off the husks of ancestors.

As I made my way back to my bedroom, I was transfixed in the dim hallway by the rows of portraits which reminded me of Claire and her paintings. The dinner, uncomfortable as it had been at times, had held the glow of family, the smooth assurance of having a place. For a moment, I allowed myself to imagine staying here forever; Fletcher would make a handsome husband, and I would grow into the lady of the household, acquire eccentricities, a flock of carrier pigeons, perhaps, or an unholy interest in heirloom tomatoes.

And then Claire again, the needle of her. I felt her laughing at the corset, the heavy oils on the walls. But surely I could rest here for a bit, shore up my strength, trade a hopeless mystery for one still alive, one that pulled at me like the pinpricks at my scalp, a dead woman calling, just close enough to discover once again.

❄

The house quieted. Thinking of Eleanor's rugs, I roused Rembrandt from his snorting sleep and led him downstairs in the dark. We felt our way, creaking along the floorboards, scraping the walls with our claws. As I had so many times over the last months, I wondered why I wasn't better provisioned. I needed a candelabra ablaze, a sidekick sleuth, a derringer, or at least a flashlight.

The front door was locked, and I couldn't see a key. Trying to remember the way to the dining room, I tugged the dog by his collar past several doorways where moonlight spilled into the hallway. As we passed one of the rooms, there was the sound of rustling, some large thing in the shadows. My heart slipped a moment, and Rembrandt let out a low woof. We passed the other doors more quickly, until I recognized the dining room.

One oil lamp still burned there, a dangerous oversight. I leaned to blow it out, and the column of heat stung my healing skin. The wick still glowed as we made our way to the swinging door to the kitchen. It was cold and smelled of dish soap and tired onions. Though the outside door was also locked, a key dangled from a hook nearby. We let ourselves out, and Rembrandt went sullenly into the snowy yard.

❄

The snow fell into the tops of the old leather boots. The silk dress dragged the ground, picking up a thick lacework of ice. It was almost unbearably cold. The yard was a long sweep of moonlight, down to the bristling black trees that surrounded the property.

There was a rushing behind me, a great sweep of air against the back of my head, an impression of heat and the smell of dust and hay. The owl, I realized as it flew past me, only inches away, its wings great arcs stretching toward the woods. I stepped backward, startled, and came up against a warm chest. Fletcher wrapped his arms around me and laughed low in my ear. "You're freezing, Henna. Why are you outside?" I gestured toward the blot that was Rembrandt further down the lawn. "You should have asked Dita to take him out," he said.

"That's hardly her job," I protested. I could feel him shrug against my back. A high warbling shriek came from the woods and was abruptly cut off. The owl was apparently quite efficient. "Why does your mother call you Franklin?"

"It's my middle name. For the past few generations, there has always been a Franklin. Tribute to the explorer."

"Did your family know him?" All my senses were on edge, trying to puzzle out the possible connections. I remembered him saying his mother's family had dabbled in shipping and worked for the Hudson's Bay Company, which had supplied Franklin's initial overland expedition.

"His wife, actually, the formidable Lady Jane. After Franklin went missing, she started up a correspondence with my great-great-grandfather, Charles Drummond." He wrapped me closer as I began to shake in the night air. "He was living in the states by that time, in this house, actually. He helped fund and staff one of her ships, but they never found anything." His voice was an odd mix of rueful and proud.

"Do you still have her letters to him?"

"They're in the collection somewhere. Undoubtedly, the connection is one of the reasons that woman decided to bring her letter here."

"Could the letter be to your grandfather? Maybe that's why she came?"

Fletcher mouth stilled against my neck. I felt his head come up. "I thought we had them all in our collection, but I suppose one could have gone missing, folded into a book that was given away or something." He rubbed his hands up and down my arms, as if checking for circulation. "It's hard to know, since we only have the two scraps, right? Since you never found any others." His hands tightened on my shoulders, and not for the first time, I regretted not telling him everything as it had happened. Now, it seemed almost farcical to admit my secretiveness, my suspicions.

"Why does your mother prefer Franklin to Fletcher?" I veered toward safer waters.

"Why not? The man whom Tennyson called 'heroic sailor soul'? My father chose my first name."

"An arrow maker." The cold was brutal. My mouth could barely form the words.

"Yes, my father had a sense of humor. Perhaps he dreamed a craftsman's life for me. A path of sober industry like his glovemaker forefathers." I tried to turn to look at Fletcher, but he held me tightly to him. "You shouldn't be out here in this weather."

"I don't suppose the Aunties' wardrobe ran to a winter coat?"

"A coat—what for? So you can run off and get yourself in trouble again?" Fletcher asked, jokingly, but with a thread of exasperation. "No, Henna, now that I have you, I'm going to keep you close." He turned me toward him, raised his hands to cup my face.

I shook him off, calling for Rembrandt. Fletcher pulled me to him by my shoulders and kissed me hard. Something flared between us, jagged and angry at first, turning softer as his mouth explored mine. I felt as if the only thing holding me up was the stiff corset. Fletcher's fingers slipped through the tear in the dress, slid over the silk of my borrowed undergarments, dug into my skin until I flinched. He drew away, set me back on my feet, both of us breathing hard.

"Your skin is so beautiful when cold, Henna," he whispered, tracing a line from my eyebrow to my jaw. I was too numb to shiver.

"All snow and ice," he said, sounding pleased. But I knew the hardness in me wasn't from the cold, was instead the shape of the black rocks that thrust from the waves near my parents' house and broke anything cast against them.

PERMAFROST

*M*OST OF ALL, SHE WISHED to go North, to see for herself. It was a constant irritation to be at the whims of men. Her niece, Sophy, told her irritants formed pearls, and Jane canceled desserts for a week. She was ill-tempered, indomitable, overbearing, canny. She would have made a fabulous explorer. Instead she navigated by the pen, by fripperies and salutations, by the great scythe of grief. She received reports from psychics who had seen her husband in his icy home. One was an old woman who stank of rotting roses. One was a witchy child in Liverpool who'd told the tale perched on her father's lap. She described the captain's cabin perfectly, recited coordinates like nursery rhymes. When Jane went to trace the bare beginnings of her husband's route, traveling no farther than Aberdeen, she was presented with blank sheets of paper in lieu of bills by the hotels. These she kept in the scrimshaw box she had intended for the reports from her husband that never came.

CHAPTER TWELVE

*D*ITA WOKE ME THE NEXT morning with a mug of hot chocolate. She bounced onto the edge of the bed, uninvited, and surveyed me. I huddled in the covers and sipped. Rich, hints of cinnamon and cayenne, Mayan, the drink of angels. "You really shouldn't have bothered," I ventured.

"But it's my job," she said with a smile. Her face was a perfect oval. Her jeans were faded at the knees and she curled her legs under her, leaning slightly against me.

"How long have you worked here?"

"Oh, Fletcher and I grew up together. My mother was the house-keeper then. I spent a few years in Bali and Nepal, trekking around, basically pretending I didn't have a family. Then my mom got sick, and I came home to help her and have been here ever since."

"I hope your mother is better now?"

"Early-onset Alzheimer's. She lives in the nursing home in the village. On very special occasions, she still remembers my name."

"I'm sorry." I shifted under the heavy coverlet. The chocolate coated my throat, too sweet now.

"Oh, you know how it is, right?" Dita flipped her hand dismissively, and I wondered what Fletcher had told her about me. She slid off the bed and went to the window to draw the curtains back. She stilled for a moment, staring down at something, then turned to me with a lovely smile, eyes alight. "Life's a bitch. I won't be the house-keeper forever, though, not like my mother."

"You like traveling too much to stay?" I thought of Dita on the beach in Bali, dancing, gold gleaming up and down her forearms.

"Something like that," she said. She reached out, and for a moment I thought she was going to stroke my arm, but instead she took the half-empty mug from me. "We've got to fatten you up," she said. The pinch was a surprise, hard on my thigh, through the covers. "Skin and bone," she mocked, tossing her hair. "Let me know when you want breakfast." She headed for the door, but turned back before leaving. "Fletcher's at the station, but he left a note for you in the study."

I threw off the covers and went to the window. Dita's perfume, full-blown roses and sandalwood, floated in the air. I saw what must have caught her attention. Two sets of footprints leading halfway down the lawn, the scuffed place at the end of them, as if a struggle had taken place, one set of prints coming back, slow marks on the snow. The memory of Fletcher carrying me, not over his shoulder as he had tussled with Dita, but in his arms, as if I were delicate.

There was a bruise on my thigh now to match the one on my hip. Quite a pair, Fletcher and Dita. I wondered what games they had played as children.

❄

Fletcher's note said, *Don't go exploring without me.* Shades of Bluebeard. Just as beguilingly handsome, I thought, as I remembered the warmth of his skin on mine last night, the shine of his hair flopping over his forehead in the moonlight, the way my bedroom felt like an underwater chamber, the two of us sipping precious air from each other until I'd pushed him out, imagining Eleanor prowling the house. It was as if the Aunties' clothing had transferred to me some lingering decorum, as persistent as the smell of cedar in the fragile silk.

Fletcher had neglected to leave a set of forbidden keys or a map to his personal den of horrors, so I disregarded his instructions and set off on a circuit of the lower level. Wings and additions had been added willy-nilly over the years. I walked through three drawing rooms, each more shabby than the last. Two doors led to narrow staircases that I ignored. In the kitchen, Dita was singing, some tribal ululation she had undoubtedly picked up on her travels, and I crept by unnoticed. There was no sign of Eleanor. Perhaps she was a late sleeper or had gone to town to plot new gazebos and attacks on presumptuous historical societies.

All the carved oak doors looked the same. I ended up back in the study, with its massive desk and blackened fireplace, several times, as if Fletcher's note were exerting a strange gravity, or as if the house was constructed as a labyrinth.

On the desk was an assortment of ornaments—pen holders, bud vases, photo frames—all made of deer hooves and bits of antler. The photos were black and white and so badly faded that the faces were featureless, pale blotches floating over rows of dark suits and dresses. On the mantel rested a pile of long bones, arranged in an indeterminate manner. One bone dangled off the edge precariously. I was glad I'd left Rembrandt shut up in the bedroom. The umbrella stand was a hollowed-out elephant's foot. A wreath of tusks made up the chandelier. The wallpaper appeared to be ostrich skin dyed dark green. Strips of it were peeling away, revealing black-streaked plaster. I fled the room, leaving the door cracked open this time so as not to be surprised again.

❄

The next time I ended up at the study, I stole a pen and the lone sheet of stationery from the desk and began to map the lower level of the house. A very domestic cartography, but still, I felt a bit of the exploring fervor as I filled in hallways and closets and named rooms for the color of their furnishings, stopping now and again to peer out the windows to orient myself. I searched for clues as I went, but there were no castoff shoes in the dead woman's size or incriminating photos or typed confessions. In the coat closet near the front door, there was a pink puffer jacket stuffed toward the back that made me wonder, and I pawed through the pockets. A scrap of paper—I felt adrift in them by this point—but not from the mysterious letter. Rather, it was blue-lined notebook paper, a raggedly torn rectangle, inscribed with rounded letters spelling out Fletcher's name and the name of our village. Below that was written *Notre-Dame-de-Bon-Secours* and an address in Montreal. Hearts and question marks were doodled around its edges, so deeply inked the paper had torn through in places. I heard Dita coming, still wailing, and barely had time to stuff the address back into the pocket before she appeared. She stopped short upon seeing me and raised a perfect eyebrow.

"Going somewhere?" she said, making it sound like a joke. I didn't know what to say and stood there rooted, holding the jacket to my middle as if covering a wound. "That's mine," she said and reached for the jacket, tugging it away from me.

The smell of frankincense arose from her like a halo, and I sneezed three times. Dita regarded me with pity as she tucked the jacket back into the closet.

"If you're truly intent on taking off, this one is more likely to fit you," she said, poking a large tweedy duster hanging from a hook on the back of the closet door. "Careful on the roads," she laughed as she swept back into the kitchen.

I waited to hear the singing start again, but all was quiet except for the hard, rhythmic sounds of a cleaver hitting board. I wondered what small creature Dita was dismembering. The makeshift map rustled in my fist, reminding me of my task.

❄

The day was dipped in pale sunlight, gleaming over the snow. From the drawing room with the burgundy curtains, I had a good view of the barn, which seemed to have been converted into a garage. The doors stood open showing two stalls, one large enough for Fletcher's pickup, the other considerably smaller, both empty. Perhaps Eleanor did not own a vehicle but was chauffeured everywhere by her dutiful son. My car still crouched in the driveway, looking quite disreputable, iced over and crusted in salt. The map of the lower level was nearly complete—only one hallway remained untried—and I was no closer to knowing if the dead woman had ever set foot here.

My mind leaped to other problems that needed solving. Last night, I'd been tempted to sink into this refuge, to play it out and see what happened, but in the light of day, the bruises still aching on my hip and thigh, I considered next steps. A contractor for my burned-out shell, someone with a backhoe and building permits to restore order to my life. Or maybe something more drastic. Ice was beginning to wear on me; perhaps I should return to the temperate ocean or one of the new Midwestern deserts, see if my hydrology skills held up away from Fletcher.

The owl flew out of the barn into the yard, a rush of grey and brown, avid hunter or restless soul, a blunted arrow.

❄

The door at the end of the final hallway led to a beautiful glassed-in passageway. A profusion of tropical plants in glazed urns and terracotta pots lined the flagstone floor. I sat on a bench carved in the shape of a Viking boat, complete with half-naked figurehead on the prow/armrest. It had started to snow again, lazy flakes sifting from a white sky. The weak sun was intensified by the multi-paned windows, and the smell of frangipani rose around me. Under cloches, orchids bloomed, perfect as paper cutouts. Glass within glass. Everything sparkled. Clearly, this part of the house received the lion's share of care.

There was a flash of movement, and I turned my head sharply, expecting to find that Dita or Eleanor had tracked me down. But it was a butterfly, tiny and powder blue. As soon as I saw it, I saw a dozen others, blue motes in the heated air. A slight disturbance, and suddenly the atrium was thick with them, flickering blue that drifted upward in a slow spiral, mirrored by the downward eddy of the snowflakes outside the glass. I was caught in the barrel of a wave, the light turned azure around me, bathed in the dust of wings. Claire's hands were always stained with her oil pastels, her fingernails filthy scraps of rainbow. What she touched, she marked. She loved the immediacy of it, whereas I had always been attracted to the painstaking tracery of water, a million years of droplets etching veins in the earth.

My mind was moving at this pace, drugged by the scent of flowers, the fog of butterflies, all my senses traveling deep into the bedrock beneath the old house, following the seep of water, beneath the lawn, under the workings of the derelict guesthouse and garden shed, flinching at the stent of the fountain plunging into the natural path of the water, feeling the tributaries joining and unjoining, gathering momentum on the far-off slopes until they ran into something too distant for me to get a good sense of, something dark and tangled, bitter as poison, a blockage that thrust back at me. I was dowsing without meaning to, a dangerous practice, a sign of a lack of control, a waking dream from which the dreamer might not break. I had just started to realize this and call my blood back, pull myself up from the slow earth, when the screaming started.

❈

I found myself on my feet at the end of the room, rattling the knob of the door there, the first locked door I had encountered. By the time I realized the screaming had been coming from the other doorway, the one through which I had entered, it had stopped. I walked cautiously through the conservatory, folding my makeshift map into quarters. The butterflies had vanished, and the snow was falling more thickly outside, turning the windows blank.

❋

Back in the main house, all was silent. I stepped carefully down a hall of doors, looking for the half-open one that would signal the study. The hallway, already dim, grew dimmer, as if someone were pulling a curtain over the house, blocking out the light. I reached out to use the wall as a guide. The map would be useless now. My hand met a doorknob, and with that slight pressure the door swung open to reveal Eleanor, her cream wool suit leached even paler by the gloom. On her shoulder was a great dark mass that shuddered and twisted until one gleaming eye revealed itself, staring directly at me.

"You heard Tiberius?" Eleanor reached up and stroked the heap of sooty feathers. The bird straightened then, twitched his wings and looked directly at me. "Black heron, very moody, this one," Eleanor murmured, smoothing the bird's neck. Tiberius turned his long beak toward her and plucked at her perfectly arranged bob.

I cleared my throat, trying to shake off the feeling of dread that had settled on me in the dark hallway. "He's lovely," I said, looking around the room. Somehow I'd missed this one in my explorations. There was a smell of ammonia and dust, and the bare wood floor was littered with feathers. The only furniture was a round table with two spindle chairs and a large rectangular black cage that spanned one corner.

Eleanor and the bird both peered at me scornfully. "He is a hunter. I'm taking him down to the cellars to feed." She walked past me, not checking to see if I followed. "We have a small riparian habitat constructed there to sustain the birds during the winter. Please close the door behind you," she said.

Of course, I thought, a riparian habitat—a necessary feature of any old Victorian house. Tiberius craned his neck, his eyes catching the barest glimmers of light.

"Would you like to join us?" Eleanor asked as she opened another of the heavy oak doors. This one revealed the top step of a staircase. The space beyond was impenetrably dark. "It can be quite educational to observe animals' behavior when they are forced out of their natural environments."

At no point in this speech did Eleanor look at me, so it was to her smooth blond head of hair that I said, "Thank you, but I'd better check on Rembrandt. He's been upstairs all morning."

Her back stiffened, and I could have kicked myself for bringing up the dog. Tiberius shifted impatiently and made a sort of hoarse growl, very different from the screaming that had broken my reverie in the solarium. "Suit yourself," Eleanor said and disappeared down the dark stairway, apparently not needing a light to guide her.

❋

Charming as the Aunties' clothing was, I figured it was high time I stepped back into my own century. And I was ready for an excursion. It was ridiculous to wander the house wraith-like, waiting for Fletcher to appear. I remembered a shop in the village called The Cozy Clothesline and foresaw a wooly sweater in my future. I nicked the tweed overcoat that Dita had suggested from the hall closet. It smelled of dead sweat and menthol, but I buttoned it securely around my antique garb. No need to give the locals more to talk about.

Rembrandt balked at venturing into the cold as I harried him into the backseat of my car, and he didn't stop snuffling and grumbling until we were away from the long driveway and headed down the hill. The ravine flashed along the edge of the road, but I couldn't spare the attention to do my own searching for the dead woman's car. My tires slipped on the snow and ice, trying to find purchase on the two narrow strips of slush that veered straight down the center of the road. I held my breath and leaned into the curves. The land around me was still and thorny, caught in a spell cast with blood, waiting for someone to blunder in and wake it.

❋

In the village, everything was closed up tight, the buildings blinking dark windows in the afternoon gloom. Only the bakery shone, and we pulled up in front of it, the sole car on the street. The three old men huddled on their bench, wheezing around cigars, wearing work gloves and deerstalkers. They barely noticed me, but tore off bits of bread for Rembrandt, who snuffled among them as if he belonged to their ranks.

The bakery was misty with steam and yeast and scents of coffee. A large man I'd never seen before leaned against the counter, laughing with the goateed barista. He had a cardboard box in his arms, and when he turned at my entrance, a spill of salt trickled from its top corner onto the rough planks of the floor. "Man, now you've done it," said the barista, "seven years bad luck."

"That's mirrors," I corrected, and the big man peered at me, before setting the box down on the counter. He bent to the floor, and I thought he was going to pluck some salt to toss over his shoulder, but instead, he cupped his hand to sweep the salt into it and dumped it into the pocket of his pea coat. "Sailors used to put sea salt in their pockets for luck before big journeys," I said, and then fell silent as both men regarded me. I felt like a girl on her first date. Or like a raven was about to come along and pluck out my eyes.

"Indeed," the big man said, almost soothingly, and held out his hand for me to shake, even though we hadn't been introduced. His palm was dry and warm, speckled with grains of salt which rolled between our joined hands like secrets we hadn't told yet. He had wild curly hair and an open smile, but as he looked at me more closely, his face began to take on the expression of a doctor about to impart bad news. Maybe it was my coat, which was exuding menthol in a faint mist. He turned abruptly back to the barista and said, "That ought to hold you a while," as he pushed the box of salt toward him. Then he went out the door without giving me another glance.

Through the fogged window, I saw him reach down to pat Rembrandt on the head and heard him laugh at something the old men offered. His laugh boomed like a gong in my veins. I bought a croissant, hot as an animal's heart, and ate it before I even got my change.

❋

I still wasn't ready to go back to Fletcher's house, and as far as I could tell, he was nowhere to be found. His truck wasn't parked on the village green, and his office was dark. I decided to visit Mariel, but on my way up the hill to her house, I saw a light glimmering in the downstairs windows of the library like a lantern on a fishing boat.

This time, I left Rembrandt in the car and threw the coat on top of him for warmth. He snuggled into it as if it were a long-lost packmate.

Harris was sitting at his desk, twirling his moustache as he read a gossip magazine. "Henna," he said as I brought the cold through the doors with me, and then chuckled at my getup. "Fancy," he said, but came around the desk to pat my arm gently. "I worried about you. Terrible thing, fire. Especially in winter." He offered tea, but I told him I had just a quick errand and that Rembrandt was waiting in the car. I snagged the key off its hook and trotted up the tower stairs as swiftly as the Aunties' skirt would allow.

My books had burned, but several of them had duplicates in the library's collection. The one I was looking for was front and center, *Arctic Exploration*, the catalogue of expeditions, the book I'd been consulting on the night of the fire—dry as dust, but comprehensive. I tamped down the memory of the sun porch blossoming. Drummond, Fletcher had said, so I started with the index, found only a Scottish botanist who had been on Sir Franklin's overland expedition in 1825. I paged through the entries of expeditions sent in search of Franklin. All those ships swarming over the icy blank, sent out by Jane Franklin in her fury and ambition. Nothing. No Drummond.

I went back again, more carefully, noting each of the expeditions in the two decades following Franklin's disappearance. There were a number of American efforts, but none mentioned Drummond. So where was Fletcher's ancestor's expedition? Perhaps I had the name wrong. I flipped to the front cover of the book—the bookplate I'd seen in so many of the collection's volumes but hadn't ever consciously noted. Donated by the Drummond Family for the Drummond Arctic Collection, copperplate scroll under a line drawing of a ship listing in the ice, its masts thrusting up bare as broken bones.

Maybe Fletcher had lied, or embellished, but to what end? I hadn't gotten the sense he was trying to impress me. Perhaps the expedition had been anonymously funded and was named after someone else, though that seemed unlikely in that era of exuberant, showy forays into the mysterious North.

Scanning the shelves, I saw nothing that promised to help pin down the ghost expedition. There were folios of correspondence, but none from the right time period. Despite Fletcher's comment about letters from Lady Jane in the collection, I couldn't find any. A quick perusal of the diaries of various explorers revealed nothing. They were all labeled as accounts of various expeditions, and again, Drummond's name did not appear. I brushed the grit from my palms, still feeling the memory of salt rolling there, and locked the room up tight again, scents of ambergris and wet wool clinging to me as I made my way back down the stairs.

Harris was locking the change drawer of the front desk. "No point in staying open. Everyone sensible is curled up with a book at home."

He perked up when I asked if I could use the computer to do a quick search, mine being incinerated, of course. As always, he hovered over my shoulder, making suggestions as I typed in "Drummond expedition" and "Arctic."

"Do you have a date?" he prompted, as I scrolled through useless links, including many for "Vanishing Arctic cruises" offered at exorbitant prices. I added "1850," but nothing fit.

"Odd," Harris said, pulling up a chair next to mine. "That Plover, remember him—fascinating guy, so well versed in esoterica. He was asking whether we had any family records for the Drummonds, same time period. I told him about the tower collection, of course, but he said he was looking for more personal material, diaries and private letters. I told him Eleanor keeps all of that stuff locked up in the old house. Well, he scurried out of here at that. Just the mention of Eleanor was enough to frighten him off," Harris chortled. "That, or he didn't want to get mixed up with a lawman. That's not a problem you have, right?"

I was starting to regret my impulse to stop by the library, but perhaps Plover offered a clue. Or maybe we were chasing the same clues, rival sleuths.

"Done here?" Harris asked, his hand on the power button. I nodded. The computer dimmed with a whine. I thought of Rembrandt in the cold car, patted Harris on his shoulder, and escaped before he could hurl any more darts of innuendo.

❄

There was no way to avoid my house on the way to Mariel's. It crouched in the darkening trees, charred and broken open, filling with white. The snow was still falling, as if it were February instead of April. Mariel seemed agitated when she opened the door, and she pulled me briskly toward the still room, not showing any surprise at my antique garb. Rembrandt followed us and flopped down at the threshold, letting out a martyred sigh when no rolls or other offerings appeared. Her jars of herbs and blossoms and pollens were a delightful mishmash of color after the bleak outdoors, and the scent of cloves and honey rose from a small enameled pot on the hotplate.

Mariel dropped my hand and dug through a cupboard in the corner. I'd never seen her so disordered. She slapped a familiar scrap of paper down on the table before me, fine linen stock, slanting black ink. At first I thought she'd rescued it from the wreck of my house, but then I read *trust you to take the greatest care* and below that *necessarily secret*. A new fragment of the letter—and one that aligned so closely with my thoughts at the library about a ghost expedition. It was as if I was pulling scraps of the letter toward me the way I used to draw water.

Mariel went back to the cupboard and returned with her notebook and silver pen. She explained she'd found it next to the beehives when she'd gone out to check them that morning before the snow started. I imagined the bees, foolishly venturing out in winter, gathering the words of a dead woman instead of pollen. But most likely it was the wind, or some grim spirit, that was seeding the woods with the letter. Or perhaps the woman had thrown them after her as she ran from whatever chased her, like breadcrumbs to mark her way.

❄

It was difficult to persuade Mariel that I would be okay at Fletcher's house. She was clearly shaken by her discovery. I regaled her with tales of Eleanor's eccentricities and Dita's barely veiled taunts and the strange furnishings. She recoiled at the description of the hooves and bones in the study and once again invited me to stay with her. It was hard to explain why I felt compelled to go back, especially while sitting in the fragrant warmth of Mariel's snug house, comforting as a cocoon. I told her how I felt the mystery unraveling, how I was sure the key to it was in Fletcher's house, how a dead woman was prodding me to play sleuth. Mariel rolled her eyes, fed me out-of-season fruit, fresh as if just picked, and touched my wrist gently in benediction. *Careful*, she signed, and slid me the scrap of letter she'd found, as if passing notes in school. I could tell she wanted it out of her house, so I took it, tucked it into the waistband of my skirt. We laughed together when she waggled her eyebrows about Fletcher. He drew me and she knew it. I told her he was like a pocket of water trapped in stone, either safe to drink or toxic, irresistible either way.

Mariel only let me leave after we'd made a plan to meet the next day at the Vanderkey house to track down Plover. I'd told her about the coincidence of him looking for the same information I was, and she expressed a desire to see that mysterious personage for herself. Rembrandt snorted at our folly and led the way to the snow-crusted car.

❄

The drive back up to Fletcher's house was perilous in the dusk. Shadows seemed to flit just outside the range of my headlights, ghosts pulling me toward the ravine. The snow pelted the windshield, and I swerved more than once as great downdrafts of wind battered us. The old car labored and slid over the shrouded road. Before long it would be impassable, and I thought again of Mariel's trepidation. But I welcomed it, being trapped in the haunted mansion, felt a grim satisfaction at throwing myself in with that hard lot. It was a test I would not shy away from. Dark recognizes dark, Claire used to say while mixing paints. I'd failed her, but my blood was stinging my veins now, just as it had on those midnight searches of the uncooperative ocean. When the black hull of the house rose suddenly before me, I almost felt like I was coming home.

❄

The barn doors were shut, so I assumed Fletcher's truck was inside. No one seemed to be around as I replaced the tweed coat in the closet and dragged Rembrandt back up to my room. The new letter fragment was rustling at my waist, and I tucked it under my pillow for safety. Downstairs, in the sitting room with the gold drapes where we had gathered the night before, I found a bookcase stocked with all sorts of sensational literature. There was a fire glowing in the hearth, and the faded brocade curtains blocked out the weather.

I curled up on one of the velvet sofas, as far away as possible from the bird cages, which were uncovered this evening. There were five of them, each holding one bird. The birds were all different, none of them the brightly colored tropical creatures I had imagined. One looked like a common crow, and his abrupt fits of coughing and cawing seemed to confirm it. The others I couldn't identify. They were medium-sized, plumed in grey and brown with slightly different-shaped heads and beaks. Now and again they rustled and clung to the sides of their cages, pecking and hissing at each other. I didn't know birds could make such sounds.

I had chosen a novel by Mary Stewart and was deep in the delicious travails of her heroine as she sped through the sun-bleached ruins of Greece when the door to the sitting room banged open. The man from the bakery hulked there, shaking his wet head like a bear, droplets spraying from his shaggy ruff.

The birds all flapped to the tops of their cages, smacked against the bars and fell to the bottoms in a cacophony of squawks. The man jerked his head around to stare at the birds and caught sight of me. What image I made in my borrowed antique clothing, which had been concealed by the coat when I'd met him earlier, I don't know, but it was enough to drain the color from his face. Looking like nothing so much as a mountain experiencing an avalanche, the man sank to the floor and lay sprawled there, motionless.

❄

I was standing over him, debating the vase full of flowers that I had snatched up versus a good old-fashioned slap, when Dita's perpetually amused voice floated from the dark hallway.

"I wouldn't," she said as she flowed into the room, graceful as a snake. "He was in Afghanistan and is still a bit jumpy." The man hadn't moved, his face buried in his burly arm. Dita nudged his side with the tip of her sneaker.

"Who is he?"

"Fletcher's cousin, Walt."

As if the sound of his name roused him, the man rolled to his side in a surprisingly quick motion and yanked at Dita's foot. She fell laughing atop him, slapping at his hands. "Brute," she said. "Behave. We have company."

Walt pushed Dita off him and lumbered to his feet, peering at me through the straggling curls that fell over his forehead. "Ah, the ghost," he said.

"This is Henna," Dita said. "Fletcher's…well, what are you, darling?" She smiled beatifically. I had a quick glimpse of worshippers clustered round her feet, proffering flesh and oil.

"Why the devil are you dressed like that?" Walt continued to glare at me.

"Her house burned down along with everything she possessed, poor thing." Apparently I was not going to be allowed to talk. "Do you recognize the Aunties' finery? It is holding up quite well, considering its advanced age," she said with another lovely smile at me.

"Were you wearing this earlier?" Walt asked, and Dita came to attention.

"Why are you so wet?" I countered. Wisps of steam rose from his coat and flicked like kisses against my skin.

"It speaks," Walt said, stepping toward me, still scowling. "The road is a mess, probably won't be plowed for a day or two. I had to leave my truck and walk the last half mile."

Trapped in the mysterious house—just as I'd hoped. Perhaps I'd been too assiduous in my gothic novel reading. I felt Claire laughing at me from far away, like a ripple moving through the bad weather. Dita pulled at Walt's arm, dragging him into the foyer, and I followed.

"You are soaked to the skin. Come with me. Your old room is still made up from last time."

"There are things I left outside that need to come in."

Dita huffed in exasperation and put on her housekeeper smile. "Yes, let me help you with your luggage," she simpered as she yanked open the coat closet. After a quick glance at me, she pulled the pink puffer jacket off its hanger and shrugged it on.

"New coat?" Walt asked, and all my senses sharpened, remembering the address in the pocket with its doodled hearts and question marks. Would Dita have Fletcher's name and directions in her pocket? Why, if she had grown up here? Perhaps it was like a teenager scrawling the name of a crush over and over, common magic. But from Dita, I'd have expected daggers and beheadings.

She thumped him on the shoulder and said, "Since when do you spend so much time thinking about ladies' clothing?" Walt shrugged, following her out into the snowy evening, where I glimpsed two bags resting on the hood of my car.

I noticed Dita didn't bother taking off the jacket when they came back inside, instead leading Walt straight back to the kitchen. I had a feeling I wouldn't see that jacket again, and I felt a tug in my gut as if hooked on a line. Perhaps I'd found something that proved the dead woman had been here after all.

The two of them disappeared down the hallway, Walt turning to crane his head back at me, Dita murmuring to him. I leaned against the front door to close it, the thick wood no defense against the cold seeping round the edges.

I went up to my room, fed Rembrandt, and fell into bed, exhausted. When I woke up, it was the middle of the night and the house was moaning in the wind. I had missed dinner and probably mortally offended Eleanor with my rudeness. Dragging the cobalt bedspread with me, I ventured to the window and saw the snow had stopped and the stars were twisting in the firmament, oblivious to any human terrors and irritations.

A good heroine would have wandered downstairs at this point, blundered into a séance or a robbery, at the very least found an ominous book of local history in the drawer of the bedside table or a bundle of bills in an antique cabinet. I kept watch on the night, listening for something, the sound of buried water maybe, hearing only the sea-floor rumblings of Rembrandt's snores.

ARCTIC HAZE

HE COULDN'T STAND BY AS his reputation grew bloodstained. Even though she knew no one would countenance it. An Englishman would hardly turn to that "last resource." The report of the bodies of thirty-five of Franklin's men found dead on the ice, next to an overturned wooden boat surrounded by bits of gold braid, a broken watch, a shotgun, and a telescope, did not convince her. There would be other explanations for the contents of the kettles at their grim camp, explanations for the wounds on the corpses, the signs of butchering. She was presented with a monogrammed spoon as proof of her husband's death. She sent more ships out in search of written record. A spoon was sorely lacking when it came to conveying crucial information.

From then on, she had two ambitions, delicately intertwined. Her husband and his crew must be shown to have been the first to complete the Northwest Passage, whether by boat or foot or mere intention, and her husband must irrefutably be proven to have died before his crew was driven to sustain itself in unthinkable ways. No longer could he be merely missing. He must be packed firm in his grave. Jane felt her mind abuzz with red and couldn't tell if it was anger or simply migraine. She took her usual cure: a dose of letter-writing, an intervention, a reshaping. Above all, she was a woman of vision; she would not rest until her way was clear.

CHAPTER THIRTEEN

I WOKE WITH MY CHEEK aching against the icy pane. The hedge was weighed down with snow, and the yard was an unbroken page glimmering in the morning light. As I came downstairs, I heard Fletcher and Dita grumbling and hissing at each other, but couldn't make out any words. Rembrandt made stealth impossible; by the time I caught up to him, Dita was shutting the door of the coat closet, her face flushed, and Fletcher had turned to greet me. He was in full uniform and held his boots in one hand.

"Our reclusive guest," he said. I realized I hadn't seen him at all the previous day. His face seemed sharper, as if he hadn't slept or eaten. He gestured me into the kitchen and shooed Rembrandt out the back door, ignoring my protests. "He can't get far," he said, and pulled a round tin and a rag from a drawer next to the sink. Fletcher unfolded a newspaper from the pile on the counter to cover the kitchen table and began to smear the black polish onto his boots. Dita plunked a cup of tea next to my elbow and glided out of the room carrying a mop and a bucket, muttering in a decidedly ungraceful manner.

"Are the roads clear, then?" I asked as Fletcher inspected his boots.

"Not really," he said. "My truck should be able to get through. Do you want to come into town with me?"

I glanced at the clock on the wall. Mariel and I had agreed to meet at the Vanderkey house at ten o'clock, and it was already eight. I didn't want to have to explain myself to Fletcher, so I said, "No, but I might try to get some exercise. Do you have snowshoes I can borrow?"

"Absolutely not. You mustn't be wandering around in this weather."

I detested being hemmed in. Everything in me rose up against it, like the water we used to set boiling in Erlenmeyer flasks in school.

Fletcher was whisking a black-bristled brush over the toes of his boots. I wondered how many hours he spent shining them, getting his uniform perfectly ironed, his felt hat free of lint and dust. For a moment, he seemed an automaton, assembled of starched twill and metal. He set down the brush and reached for my hand.

"I worry for you, Henna. You have a propensity for trouble. Promise you'll stay here where I know you'll be safe."

I wondered how long he thought it would take, for me to be safe. I yanked my hand away from his. His teeth glinted as he grasped my wrists to pull me toward him, across the table, ignoring the over-turned cup of tea. A sharp yelp at the door intervened, and I got up to let Rembrandt in.

"Promise me, Henna. No excursions." His goodbye kiss smelled of shoe polish and newsprint, and I didn't bother to cross my fingers when I replied.

❉

Unsurprisingly, Dita was eager to usher me out into the cold. The snowshoes she produced were wooden with rawhide lacing and as out of date as my attire. Regretfully, I shut Rembrandt in my room. I was already running late and didn't have time for canine hijinks in the frozen woods. I was bundled again in the tweed coat. As I'd guessed, the pink puffer jacket was no longer in the closet. There was also no sign of Walt or Eleanor. With no other options for directions, I asked her how to get to the Vanderkey house, feigning an interest in local architecture. Her attention sharpened then, and she cocked her head to the side, considering me. The small feathers in her hair and the smear of grime across her T-shirt did nothing to blunt her malice.

"Why not?" she said. "Good luck finding it in this weather." She pointed me across the road, saying there was a stream I could follow that skirted the base of the hill between the two houses. It was obvious that she thought I'd get lost and be back in short order, or better yet, disappear forever. But she didn't know about my dowsing, and she underestimated the lure of my curiosity.

By the time I left the house, clumsily adjusting my stride to the awkward snowshoes and the bulky coat and skirt, I was running late. The snow was deep, and I sank into each step once I'd crossed the road. I felt for the hidden stream. It was a strand of electricity before me that I followed as surely as blood travels a vein. Ravens flew overhead to the submerged cornfields, braying with anticipation. The clouds shifted and cleared, building up mass. In the sunny moments, the glare was unbearable. I covered my eyes with my fingers, squinting through the slits, imagining old Arctic explorers with their rudimentary sun goggles, leather or wood or bone, scored with slits and crosses.

Clouds, more clouds, then the house, perched halfway up the far side of the hill. I'd probably only gone two miles, but it felt like it had taken forever, and I looked around for Mariel, hoping she hadn't been waiting long. The house seemed deserted, driveway unplowed, the front steps thick with snow. It was a more modest mansion than Fletcher's, and better kept: pristine white siding and restrained gingerbread and charcoal shutters, a new slate roof and shining weathervane with a proud rooster perched mid-crow. Mariel was nowhere to be seen. There were no marks in the snow except mine. Since the road seemed impassable, she would have to snowshoe or ski across the ravine. I made a circuit of the house—no car, no sign of life—but as I came around the back, I saw a plume of steam rising from the furnace pipe. Someone was home.

When I returned to the front, the ring I'd trudged in the snow like a protective circle around the house was complete. I stepped inside of it, laboriously removed the antique snowshoes. I stamped my feet, knocking off as much snow as I could. As if he'd been waiting for that sign, Plover opened the door wide.

"Henna, lovely lady of the library, what a surprise," he exclaimed, gesturing me inside and tugging at my coat. It was warm in the house, almost tropical. I relinquished the tweed and stood dripping onto the varnished concrete floor. The Vanderkey house had been renovated extensively. Although the outside was traditional Victorian, the inside had been gutted and whitewashed, transformed into a cavernous open space with low-slung canvas couches and brightly painted masks on the walls. Stainless steel counters and appliances gleamed in the exposed kitchen. Mariel was not there. Plover wore a pair of silk pajama pants, striped yellow and turquoise, and a garish oversized Fair Isle sweater that could only have come from the shop down in the village.

"Will you join me for tea? Or something stronger? Though I must say I'm running a bit low on that sort of supply. May I fetch you a towel? And a seat? A blanket? The weather in this place is too terrible to be believed." He left no space for answers, which was a relief, since I hadn't planned how to explain my uninvited presence. As he spoke, he shepherded me toward the canvas couch and plopped down next to me. "Dear girl, what a delight! I'm moldering here, so far away from everything, stuck in this ridiculous house, and the phones and wireless down. I've turned to books, if you can believe it, but the owners seem to read only horror or Civil War histories."

It was clear no uncomfortable questions were going to be asked about my showing up on his doorstep. When he wound down his scathing review of the accommodations, he leapt up to rummage through the kitchen, returning with a half-empty bottle of sherry and two asymmetrical stemless glasses. They listed precariously on the giant slab of redwood that stood in for a coffee table. "This is what I'm down to," he caroled, "like an old lady in a country-house novel."

Plover fluttered and hovered, dipped from one end of the room to the other like a top-heavy moth, bringing me more cushions, a bowl of picked-over nuts, a glass of water to accompany the sherry. Sweat was rolling down my back. The house was hollowed out, two stories tall in the living room, with a precarious-looking balcony up above. Two large skylights shed weak light over the couches. The clouds were still building. The masks on the walls were forbiddingly jubilant, wide mouths open in acrylic grimaces.

"Let me guess, my dear. You came to learn more about my little museum? Perhaps you have something you'd like to show me, something handed down from a family member? Or something you've found in your travels?"

I recoiled, my mind superimposing the shrouded figure of the dead woman over an image I remembered from Plover's website, the embalmed whale rolling helplessly alongside the aircraft carrier.

"Not at all," I insisted primly, channeling the governess I was dressed as.

Plover landed next to me and snatched up his sherry. "I'm intrigued. What can I do for you?" He infused the question with all the plummy solicitousness of a born showman, the kind whose hands you should keep an eye on.

"Harris at the library told me we are researching the same thing, and I thought we might pool our resources," I began, sipping at the sherry cautiously. Burnt raisin and butterscotch pudding, overlaid with a strong patina of dust. "The Drummond Expedition of the 1850s," I added.

It was a shot in the dark. Plover's reaction was gratifyingly dramatic. He stilled as if pinned in place. Then he gulped his sherry and said, "Never heard of it, I'm afraid."

"But Harris said…"

Plover set his glass down hard and patted my thigh with his plump hand. "Mistaken, my dear. I cast a wide net when I'm looking for new specimens, but most leads don't pan out. Some things just aren't worth the trouble." His patting was growing more frantic. I gently relocated his hand to his own leg.

"Fletcher mentioned the Drummond expedition to me. Maybe he talked with you about it, too?" I persisted.

"Our gallant police chief?" Plover inquired. "Barely know him, not well anyway." His glasses were fogging in the humid air. "But I have all kinds of delights I could show you, many I've collected from right around here. A whole drawer of arrowheads, limestone and chert, some beautiful quartzite. A cache of what might be the last dwarf wedge mussels, very interesting mating habits those. And a huge *Coluber constrictor* skin, intact, must be five feet at least." He rose, presumably to find these treasures.

"Wait," I said, clutching his arm. "I think it may have something to do with the woman who died in the woods. She was carrying a letter that seemed to make reference to an old Arctic expedition."

Plover looked at me, perhaps with pity; it was hard to tell with his clouded glasses. "I'm sorry you were the one who found her. It is never easy to be the witness, is it?"

He smoothed the front of his sweater fretfully. I noticed that woven into the pattern were lynxes and cranes, sea turtles and spider monkeys, a knitted litany of vanished creatures.

He enveloped me in a damp hug, taking me by surprise. Against my hair, he whispered, "You must be careful. Like I said, some pursuits aren't worth the risk."

"How so?" I demanded, pulling away.

He ignored me, pointing upward. "My dear, not to be inhospitable, but you might wish to set off again. Your house is all the way across the ravine, am I right?"

The skylights were darkening, filling with the heavy snow that had been falling for some time without my noticing it.

"My house burned down, so I'm staying just over the hill, at Fletcher's."

Plover startled and stepped back, stumbling against the coffee table. "But you should not be there. Not *there*, of all places," he said.

No matter how much I pressed him, he would say no more. Eventually, I took pity on him and left. As I fastened the snowshoes, the windows began to glow, and I could see Plover flitting from light to light, igniting them against the gathering dark.

❄

Even though it was barely midday, the storm had descended with a gloom that cast the landscape into shadow. The snow fell thickly as I broke through the protective circle and followed my own blunted tracks back to Fletcher's. At least I'd learned one thing. Plover had known nothing of my house burning down, which seemed to exonerate him of that deed. But it was also clear he had a better acquaintance with Fletcher than he'd wanted to let on, and whatever it was he knew, it scared him.

I trudged back to the place where I thought I needed to veer toward the road. I could see nothing in the storm. But I felt the thread of the stream to my right and a bit ahead of me, not far now, the pockets of water that must signal Fletcher's house. I thought briefly of Mariel snug at home and didn't worry for her. Unlike me, she was undoubtedly too smart to venture out in such weather.

I was still shaken by Plover's reactions. What had Fletcher done to frighten him so? Or maybe it was one of the other denizens of the house Plover was trying to warn me away from. Dita with her cruel fingers, or Eleanor with her birds.

A raven flew up out of the brush at me, black slash across my vision. I reared back, lost my footing, and tumbled down the side of the hill, into the shallower snow of the road, and came up hard against something that materialized into a tire, incongruous and solid as a kiss.

❄

At first, I had the wild idea that I'd found the dead woman's car, but then a large hand reached down and yanked me to my feet. The snowshoes had been torn off somewhere in the fall, and I abandoned them to their fate. Walt brushed at the tweed coat ineffectually until I pushed him away and shook myself all over like Rembrandt, dislodging most of the snow. Not that it mattered. The flakes were still falling densely around us, burying his truck even more thoroughly.

He called over the wind, "Why are you out here without a hat?" He shifted the large paper-wrapped package he was lugging under one arm and steered me toward Fletcher's house. In the entry, we left great pools of meltwater on the floors, and I imagined Dita's exasperation. The house was very dark. Walt and I stood quiet as children dared to spend the night in a haunted mansion.

With that thought, the clocks started ticking again and the sound of high heels clicked toward us. Walt moved toward the kitchen with his bundle. I put away the wet coat and ran upstairs before Dita or Eleanor could appear to taunt me about all the things I had lost.

❄

In the gloom of my bedroom, I patched the blue silk dress. Someone, probably Dita, had left a small basket of sewing supplies on my perfectly made bed. The kit looked ancient, like everything else in the house, and consisted of a crumbling cardboard packet of needles, a faded pink velvet pin cushion in the shape of a heart, and several skeins of thread, all dark colors. None matched the dress exactly. The snow was a film blinding the windows, and Rembrandt rolled on the rug, dreaming of furry things in burrows, good places to dig and piss and lick. Far away, the slam of a door, a cascade of chimes, the croaks and coughs of caged things. Fletcher or Eleanor must have emerged. From the bathroom, all the mirrors glimmered and winked at me until I got up and pulled the door closed.

I'd never been a good seamstress. The thread, purple as a pansy in the shade, slick as a drowned maiden's hair under my fingers, formed a lumpy tendril on the silk.

❄

That night, dinner was lamb, tender as the elusive spring. The formal table had reclaimed the center of the room and was set in layers of china and silver and damask linen. Bowls of peas and creamed spinach, great fluffy swaths of potatoes, and crisp greens swam up and down its length as we passed things to one another, politely, impeccably, orchestrated as a country reel.

I ventured a compliment to Dita on her cooking and her laugh rang forth. "All Walt's doing," she grinned, nudging his shoulder. "He's a traditionalist." She was dressed in a shrunken Sex Pistols T-shirt and skin-tight leggings, feet bare again, a funeral pyre's worth of bracelets clattering on her forearms. Walt grunted and spooned up more potatoes. "You know, back to the land, locavore kind of stuff," she said. "My tastes are more exotic." I could have sworn she winked at Fletcher, but perhaps it was the candles flickering.

"It's nice someone could make use of the old homestead, though why you abandoned medicine, I'll never know," Eleanor proclaimed, brushing at her aqua sweater. A small black feather rose from her and hovered over the heat of the table.

"Do you live nearby?" I asked Walt.

He shook his big head a few times as if shrugging off drops of water. I was back in the blue silk, the vein of purple thread hard against my hip. Perhaps he still thought me ghostly, because he looked just to the side of me as he answered. "A couple of hours upstate, actually. I have a restaurant there, and a farm stand in the summer, and some college kids who help out on breaks." He shoveled more food into his mouth and leaned forward on his elbows, peering intently at his plate.

Dita laughed again. "And a kitchen shop and an online catalog and a cookbook. Our Walt here is a celebrity. He owns half that town, has it all painted up, signs with antique fonts—the blacksmith's shop selling artisanal breads, moonshine in the old gas station, twenty-four dollars a jar, a barber with mutton chops who'll shave you with a straight blade."

"Yes, Walt, don't hide your light under a bushel," Fletcher drawled, leaning back in his chair, tipping on its two spindly legs. His cream fisherman's sweater was immaculate, his hair more golden than ever, as if he had spent the day in the sun. "Speaking of your many enterprises, did you bring us our quarterly rations?"

Dita explained, "Walt keeps the deep freeze stocked with meat and Eleanor's birds in fleshy bits."

"So kind," Eleanor murmured, with a moue of distaste, though she was forking up the lamb readily enough, her rings glinting.

"Carried it in from the pickup today," Walt said, dragging bread through gravy. "Henna helped."

"So you had an excursion after all, Henna?" Fletcher looked amused.

Dita said, "That's right. Did you find the Vanderkey house?"

Fletcher's chair thumped back onto all four legs with a crash. The remaining lamb trembled on its platter. Eleanor reached out to touch his hair, gold on gold, and the house shuddered and went dark.

❋

After a pause, our eyes adjusted. The candles still shimmered, but the room was already noticeably colder, and the house made a whistling sound as if deflating. From outside came the sound of howling, the wind flying in a pack. We were all silent, waiting, until Fletcher sighed, pushed back his chair and said, "That damn generator."

Dita hopped up and crossed to him, placing her hand on his arm. "Do you want help?"

"I'll take Henna. She hasn't had a tour of the cellars yet."

Eleanor said, "She's hardly dressed for it."

"Ah, she'll do," Fletcher tugged me up by the wrist. I dropped my fork and it clanged loudly on my plate, causing Eleanor to wince and Dita to laugh again. Walt sat back from the table, shadowed, drawn into himself as if weathering something unpleasant. He didn't offer to accompany us.

❄

Fletcher snatched a candlestick bearing three tapers from the sideboard and led the way down the black hallway. As we skirted the main staircase, I rammed my hip painfully into the scaled finial at the bottom and yelped. From upstairs, I heard a faint answering bark from Rembrandt. "Maybe I should go check on him," I ventured, not any more desirous of seeing the cellars than I had been the day before.

"He'll be fine," Fletcher said and slipped down the hallway, taking with him the halo of light.

"Don't you have one of those big metal flashlights, something with twenty batteries and lots of lumens?" I asked as I caught up.

"Yes, but that wouldn't be any fun, would it?" He was at the door to the cellar, and as he opened it, a gust of damp air whooshed out. It smelled of bird droppings and marsh. I grabbed a fistful of his sweater at the small of his back, unwilling to be stranded in the dark. "The generator is supposed to come on automatically, but it's a bit glitchy. It's right near the bottom of the stairs," he said as he proceeded downward. "Would you like to go first with the light?" He stopped, and I ran into his broad back. His briny, smoky smell surrounded me.

"I'd never get round you without falling down the stairs."

"Did you find the Vanderkey house?" he asked, not moving.

I debated lying to him, remembering Plover's alarm at hearing where I was staying.

He must have taken my silence for assent. "Was anyone home?"

"Plover was there," I said. "Remember the man with the strange museum?"

"I remember Plover." He was very still.

"He seemed upset when I mentioned I was staying here."

He moved forward so abruptly that I almost fell. I reached for the walls, finding them closer than expected, giving me the vertiginous feeling that the stairway was stretching ever narrower, closing on us.

"Plover is…imaginative. Unstable."

He held the candles high so that the light spilled back to me, and I hurried to catch up. At the base of the stairs, he stopped again, turning in a circle to illuminate the space. I caught a glimpse of a curtain of black trash bags and a pile of stainless steel bowls, presumably for the birds.

The lower half of Fletcher's face was in shadow as he leaned toward me. "I want you to stay away from Plover."

I would have expected nothing else, but I flinched at his vehemence. "Why?"

"Let's just say he is a person of interest, and I don't trust him."

"You think he had something to do with the dead woman? So, she didn't just wander into the woods and die of exposure?"

"Why don't you leave the investigating to me? You poking every hornet's nest can only lead to trouble." He moved closer. I couldn't tell if he was amused or angry.

"You think he was the one trying to scare me off with the library and the fire?" I suddenly remembered Plover's casual knowledge that I lived across the ravine.

"I'm not sure yet, but I like having you where I can keep an eye on you." Fletcher was still advancing, eerily shadowed. I retreated toward the stairs until I ran out of space.

"You're not frightened, are you?" he asked, mockingly, and blew out the candles.

❄

At first there was silence, thick enough to choke me, and then, faintly, the plashing of water, and incongruously, the chirping of frogs and insects. It might have been a summer night, dank and humid, smelling of wet dirt and animal droppings. I reached out for Fletcher, but he was gone.

❄

I did not call out, but rather moved forward, my hands outstretched, toward my memory of the black plastic curtain. It crinkled as I came up against it. I pushed it aside and there was a rattling of squawks and trills, the sense of large forms moving in the damp gloom, a fetid smell underlying everything—something rotting down here, some prey saved for later.

I reached out to the water as if to a map and felt the sheen of it on the walls, the trough of it in the middle of the long room, sacs of it in the small shapes of frogs and crickets, and then the bigger bulbous hearts of the birds, arrayed all around, some perched high, some crouched by the artificial river. And a few feet in front of me, a mass of veins and organs, cold blood pulsing. I stretched to touch Fletcher with fingertips made electric with the dowsing and he jumped back an inch, said, "Henna, what are you doing?" and then surged forward and wrapped me in his arms.

I pulled myself back into my own skin, the feel of his mouth on mine, the rush of my own blood that was circling like an animal trying to escape. I wondered how far he would go. We were caught together, his hands rough on my body, his teeth at my throat, and then there was a wet sound as the silk of the dress ripped again, this time along the bodice, and we pulled apart, sightless in the dark.

"Ah, Henna, you're killing me." There was a click, then a roaring hum, and a clutch of colored spotlights popped on, each hidden in a clump of greenery around the small stream. A pump started up and the water flowed; a snapping turtle leapt off a rock and disappeared. The house groaned and creaked as the heat came back on. I thought I heard Dita's shriek of laughter from above. Fletcher stood there, hands in his pockets. "Mother will not be happy," he said, and I looked down to see the whole front of the beautiful blue dress torn, corset exposed, fabric sheared as if by talons.

❄

"Grand tour?" Fletcher asked, gesturing down the length of the room.

Grateful for the change of subject, I followed as he picked his way along the artificial stream. The croaks of toads and chittering of insects rose around us. The birds remained hidden, but they rustled disapprovingly. Mosquitoes whined around my ears and rust-colored geckos darted across the path.

"What kind of birds does your mother keep?"

"Carrion birds. Raptors. She likes the carnivores." We had almost reached the end of the stream, where it trickled into a rock-circled pond, surrounded by troughs of ferns and rubber plants. "When I was a child, she told me ancient peoples worshipped the hunter birds because they carried the dead to the top of this world and into the next. There was one story about a crow that got so cold as it made the journey all of its feathers turned white." He felt along the wall at the end of the room, and there was a rattle of a lock as a door swung open. The room grew markedly cooler, and Fletcher ushered me past him, into a frigid dark space. Once I stepped inside, an overhead fluorescent light automatically clicked on. He followed me, pulling the door closed behind us.

❄

The room was lined with large industrial freezer units that looked like small shipping containers. There must have been seven or eight of them, all hooked up with thick cords to car batteries, as well as plugged into the hefty sockets that ringed the walls. Three generators growled in the corners. Fletcher stood squarely in the middle of the room, thumbs tucked into his pockets, and raised his eyebrows at me.

"The birds' provisions?" I wondered just how many birds Eleanor had.

"Nope."

"You're a serial killer?" This came out a bit less playful than I'd hoped, but he laughed and reached out to draw me with him to the nearest unit. It had a fan in the center of its metal face and a solid door fastened with an elaborate latch and a padlock. He worked the lock with one hand, keeping hold of me with the other.

When the hatch popped open, a rush of plastic-smelling air escaped in a blast of vapor. He gestured for me to look inside. In the middle of the compartment lay a single irregular hunk of cloudy ice, the size of a cinder block. The center of the ice was bruised faintly turquoise.

"The Macculloch Glacier on Baffin Island. What remains of it, anyway." He swung the door shut and refastened the lock.

"I don't understand." My mind sorted through a catalogue of Arctic formations, accrued in my time of stocking the encyclopedia. "That glacier melted two years ago."

"Yes, and this is the last bit of it, harvested six months before it disappeared for good."

"So, these are all dead glaciers?" I gestured to the other freezers.

"Most of them." He pointed to the unit closest to the door. "That one holds core samples from existing glaciers and local snow specimens."

A sadness hung in the room, as if these shards of ice were wild things sedated and caged.

"How do you get them?"

"Some of them, I gathered myself. Some of them, I've bought from enterprising adventurers over the years." He grinned at my expression. "I told you I came from a long line of collectors."

"It must cost a fortune to keep them."

"It's an expensive hobby." Fletcher rubbed his fingers over my knuckles, warming one small line of me.

I looked suspiciously at Fletcher. "Why are you the police chief? You clearly don't need the job."

"Civic duty." He released my hand, and I walked around the room, shivering, touching the metal doors one by one. The mosquito that rode in on my bare shoulder fell to the ground. Perhaps it was too cold for it. Perhaps my blood was poison.

"What will you do with all this?"

"Some of it is sold already. Some of it I'll keep."

"Sold?"

"To Plover," he growled. I jumped, feeling vaguely guilty. "For his museum."

I imagined that ship of lost things sitting low in the water, waiting for Plover to return laden with new treasures. I could not stop trembling. Fletcher stripped his sweater off and settled it over my shoulders so that his warmth mantled me as he led the way out. The humid environment of the birds' hunting grounds was a shock, the air so thick it was hard to breathe, but I kept Fletcher's sweater tucked around me. As we navigated the stream, brushed through the plastic curtain, and started up the stairs, I couldn't shake the feeling that we were climbing into another world, and that we'd left the real one below us buried in the hum of generators.

❄

All that ice melting, giving up its lost bodies, corpses strewn across the landscape, leathered by the cold, the bones with their marks of butchery. Offering up larger prizes, also, like Franklin's ships, incredibly preserved by the cold water. I'd seen the photos of items recovered from the wrecks—a pair of blue spectacles tinted against the glare of everlasting sun on snow, a seal fur–lined slipper, intact willow pattern plates, the ship's bell, lime kelp spilling from it. Perhaps it was no wonder I still had hopes of the sea releasing its stolen treasures.

So much water to be plumbed though—best to stay firmly pinned to the mystery close at hand. Which made me think again of the ghost expedition and Jane Franklin writing *necessarily secret.* Why? Arctic expeditions were by their very nature meticulously recorded and the source of public interest. Hiding a journey would defeat its purpose: the goal of pushing outward into that blank terrain, filling it with maps and measurements.

The stairs were only dimly lit, even with the generator running. I touched Fletcher's back as we climbed and considered how to ask him again about his ancestor, wondering if there had already been enough revelations for one night. Then we were at the doorway and he was shoving through it, and the house sighed at our entry, as if welcoming a lost love.

❄

"Speak of the devil," Fletcher said viciously, as we emerged from the hallway into the foyer. Plover stood there, dripping onto the ornate rug.

"My favorite police chief," he exclaimed, advancing on Fletcher with his hands outstretched.

Even after Fletcher's warning, I still couldn't bring myself to be scared of Plover. His down parka was lime green and his cap hunter orange. He was wearing snowboarding pants patterned in acid-yellow camouflage. A bulky pair of lavender ski goggles dangled from one wrist. He grabbed Fletcher's shoulders in a half hug and then turned to me, eyeing the bodice of my dress with concern. I pulled Fletcher's sweater over my head to put it on properly.

"You remember Henna?" Fletcher said, testing him.

"Of course," Plover said, clasping my hand through the dragging sleeve of the sweater. "Beautiful Henna, angel of the library. We met last week."

"More recently than that, surely?" Fletcher said, his voice as harsh as I'd ever heard it.

Plover paled, but he summoned a smile when Dita ambled into the room, bracelets jangling. He swept the orange cap off his head and sank into a deep bow, the wing of his hair flopping forward and settling back as he straightened.

"Dita, my dear, love of my life, I haven't seen you in weeks. You are more radiant than ever. When will you accept my offer to run away with me? Leave these humble folks to their snow. We shall search out a tropical island where I shall fatten you on dates and coconuts as we brown ourselves in the sun."

Plover's rhapsody came to a halt as Eleanor materialized from the shadows behind Dita.

"What are you doing here?" Eleanor asked, regarding him even more coldly than she did Rembrandt.

"I came to borrow a cup of sugar. My stores are running low." Plover shook off his jacket and stamped his boots firmly on the oriental carpet, avoiding looking in my direction. "And if you wanted to throw in a couple of bottles of wine to go along with the sugar, that would be smashing."

"How did you get here? The roads are blocked." Eleanor advanced upon him as if to push him back out the door.

"Snowmobile. Wondrous contraption. Too loud though, my ears are still ringing."

Fletcher sounded angry as he said, "You shouldn't use the snowmobile in the dark. It's a fool's mistake."

Plover glared. "I can't be expected to stay cooped up in that house all the time. You are being unreasonable." Then he glanced at me and his face smoothed out. He added in his showman's voice, "I'm a sailing man. I can't be kept landlocked for so long. It's not good for my lungs." He thumped his chest. "Nor my digestion." He patted his rotund belly. "Nor any number of my other parts," he concluded grandly, gesturing with a flourish to his lower half.

At this juncture, Walt straggled from the hallway, blinking at Plover's attire.

"Ah, another guest," Plover clapped his hands. "Fresh company, a fellow traveler, new meat." Walt was impervious to this outburst, and no one offered to introduce the men. "C.C. Plover, at your service." Walt's hand was captured in both of Plover's, but it barely moved as Plover attempted a vigorous shake. "Big fellow, aren't you?"

❄

Somewhere outside, the owl screamed. White feathers rustled in the hedge. Across the snow, a woman wrote in silver and cupped jars of honey in her palms to warm them. Between the owl and the good witch, something lay buried. I could almost feel it, the blank metal of the woman's car, trapped like a rowboat. Nine lemon pips burrowed into the frozen earth, taking their chances.

❄

Fletcher led us all into the sitting room, seemingly resigned to Plover's presence. A cabinet in the corner opened to reveal a shelf of bottles and an array of glasses. Without asking for anyone's preferences, he began pouring out amber liquid and passing it round. The bourbon was peppery and blazed on the way down. We arranged ourselves on the sofas and chairs, silently, as if preparing for a trial. Dita looked amused as ever, flopping full length across a brocade lounge.

We all turned at the sound of a cough coming from the depths of the room. Only one of the cages was occupied. It held a large reddish-brown bird with white patches on its cheeks and a strongly hooked beak. It coughed again, then rustled the feathers of its ruff, not taking its eyes off of us.

"A Madagascar fish eagle." Plover sounded reverent as he approached the cage, drink in hand. "There are only three of these left in the world." He turned accusingly to Eleanor. "How did you come by him?" Eleanor didn't bother to reply, and Plover turned back to the bird and extended a finger to the cage, as if to stroke his plumage.

"Are you offering to feed Vedius this evening? Your hand would hardly be a snack." Eleanor sounded more pleased than she had all night as she rose to join Plover. She rummaged in a bin by the cages and came up with a fawn leather gauntlet, which she held up to Plover. He seemed tempted, but shook his head. She snaked it on over her rings and up past the sleeve of her cashmere sweater. The cage door opened with a clang and Eleanor leapt, whip-quick, to thrust her arm beneath the bird, who hopped readily onto it and gripped it with his strong feet as she brought him out into the room.

The bird turned its head from side to side, pinning each of us with its glare. Fletcher refilled Plover's drink, then capped the bottle of bourbon and drank deeply from his glass. I noticed Walt hadn't touched his.

"They are rare in that they take fish from the surface rather than diving," Plover said.

"And in that there are only three remaining," Walt murmured.

"That, too," Plover said brightly. "Gorgeous isn't he? And how can we measure how much of his beauty is due to his scarcity? His eventual disappearance hangs over him like a glamour."

Fletcher twitched at this poetic sentiment and stepped away from the cabinet. Eleanor warned, "No sudden movements," as the bird flared its wings and settled again, head pivoting.

Plover continued, undaunted. "He will be even more exquisite when he is the only one of his kind left." He glanced at me as he said this, perhaps hoping for encouragement, but my tolerance for grandstanding was already at its limit. "This is what I'm trying to preserve in my museum: the allure of the final specimen, its pathos and grandeur. Just last week I obtained the skin and skull of the last northern white rhino. They were shipped to me overnight from Kenya. Across the ocean and through a snowstorm." He shook his head in wonder. "Progress," he enthused. "I have a whole room full of salamanders on my ship, amphibians are expiring at such a rapid rate. The botanical wing is also filled. The last crates of natural silk ever spun are in transit to me right now. We are living at a historic juncture, the brink of another mass extinction, and we are rushing toward it like starving people, cannibalizing our children and our children's children."

I jumped at mention of cannibalism, the line of fallen explorers springing to mind. Fletcher's mouth tightened. The bird shifted restlessly, but Eleanor held her arm steady, perfectly parallel to the floor, indicating a strength I hadn't guessed.

Dita laughed and raised her glass, "To annihilation, then. The sooner, the better."

Plover drained his drink. "This is what I'm saying—even the young are pessimists. But we will all grow old before our time and become nostalgic, and then those that are left will flock to my museum to relive the war we waged with our future and lost." He garbled these last words. Fletcher watched him closely. Plover choked out, "So much splendor, these bright end years." And then he fell into Eleanor, jolting her, and the bird took off, swooping swiftly around the room as Plover collapsed to the floor.

Dita shrieked and Eleanor barked an angry, indecipherable curse. Fletcher seemed frozen in place. I felt paralyzed, but Walt calmly raised his arm and the bird came in for a landing, as if they were long-time hunting partners. All of its feathers spread and sleeked, pulse of a dying world. Eleanor hustled forward, gauntlet outstretched. She retrieved the bird to bundle it back into its cage.

❀

Fletcher had knelt beside Plover and was prodding his neck and chest. "Drunk," he proclaimed. Dita laughed. The bird, resituated on its perch, called loudly, a series of piercing cries like a lost child. Walt came to help me up from the couch. If it had not been for the blood running down his wrist, we never would have guessed he was injured.

❀

I was elected to bandage Walt, and despite his protests, I bathed the deep gouges in his forearm in the bathroom off the foyer and found a box of gauze in the medicine cabinet above the sink to bind his wounds. The two of us could barely fit in the small room. Walt sat on the toilet and I stood between his legs, my movements hampered by the rigid corset and Fletcher's sweater.

Exasperated, I stripped off the sweater, forgetting the ruin of my bodice. Walt pressed his lips together until they whitened. He blurted, "What are you doing here, Henna?" and clasped my shoulder. I felt that if I stood there long enough, exactly like this, with his hand on my skin, I could finally get warm. Fletcher flashed through my mind, but this was a different kind of heat, the steady burn of a woodstove or a lamp in the dark.

The makeshift bandage flapped over his arm, and I turned from him to fiddle with the first-aid supplies. Behind me, Walt exhaled in frustration, and I looked back to see his palms pressed hard to his eyes, as if trying to block out the sight of me. Then he got up and gently pushed around me to head upstairs.

I followed, skirting the doorway of the sitting room, where Fletcher, Dita, and Eleanor were dealing with Plover. I heard Eleanor proclaim, "He should never have come back here. He knew the agreement."

Dita broke in, amused, "But did you have to do such a good job of it? He'll be hell to lift."

"I'll take care of it, Mother," Fletcher said in low, calm tones. "I'll get him home tonight, and that will be the end of it. He can send for the specimens from his ship." Fletcher in his own domain was proving to be rather unsettling.

"I call the feet," Dita said gaily, and I scurried to the stairs before they could appear with their cargo. In the hallway, I stopped to catch my breath. My list of suspects was growing gratifyingly, and I felt more alive than I had in a year.

The bird's shrieks tore through the house in counterpoint to the clocks chiming. Midnight again, witching hour, hinge of the day, time when a twin could call to her sister's shade, if she knew how. I concentrated. My senses spread out, like rings in a pond, but the house was too solid, bound upon itself like a ship provisioned for a half-dozen winters, and around it fell the snow, an unbreachable static.

CICATRIX

As the scurvy took hold, teeth started to fall out. The fingernail beds wept. Some men saw visions, a door in the ice, a hand reaching for them at night. Old wounds, healed years ago, reopened. The men were bleeding their histories. Brawl at the Black Bottle, lamp oil explosion, bite from a childhood dog. The smile across his palm where the knife slipped when slicing an apple. The flesh of the fruit was paper thin, rimmed in gold. He fed it to her piece by piece as she lay on the divan, silk on silk, pink opening to deeper pink. Black seeds tumbling to the floor. The way she went still when he touched her and then even more still. Holding their breath, both of them. Him with the knife yet in his hand. His fingers sticky. The juice was running now, sweeter than he had expected. The flesh was easily bruised. He cut away the bad parts and gave her the rest. The world shrank down to the size of a pip and then expanded again—a bud, a flower, fruit so heavy it drops. She recoiled when she saw the blood. Her dress was ruined, her hair undone. Here, on the ship, embraced by the ice, the blood came again, swam up in long-forgotten scars to chart their little injuries, their cherished pain.

CHAPTER FOURTEEN

*T*HE NIGHT WAS SPENT LISTENING to the wind tearing around the casements. The scrap of letter under my pillow was a pebble in the bed. I'd dreamt a dead woman whispering to me and men with blackened faces pulling a wooden boat and Mariel's bees crisping in their boxes.

I woke feeling encased in wax, deadened by the endless cold and the gray sky that blocked the window. But as I thought about all I'd discovered so far, my blood heated. Plover had been here arranging to buy the glaciers and then had been confined to his house on Fletcher's orders. Had he seen the woman that night? The pink jacket flashed into my mind. What had Plover witnessed that made Eleanor and Fletcher so intent on muzzling him? Was Plover really as dangerous as Fletcher had implied, when he did his best in the cellar to shock me with his rough handling? I was beginning to feel I'd stepped into a snare and the lines were pulling tight.

The hedge outside the window felt like a dark border. Something drew me to it. I'd learned to trust my intuition over years of hunting water, and I resolved to take Rembrandt out for a closer look. What other secrets did the house hold? If I was inside the trap, I might as well make the most of it. I remembered my makeshift map and the peculiar gravity of the study, how it had drawn me again and again. I shuddered at the memory of the animal parts that littered it. And the volumes lined up like gravestones on the dusty shelves—the family records? Perhaps the proof of Drummond's mysterious expe-

174 • TINA MAY HALL

dition had been before me all along. A thread was emerging here, a pathway to follow. Grief had made me reckless. I was no longer an easy person to deter, especially with the dead woman pulling at me like a sister.

Dita did not appear with chocolate and taunts, so I braved the chill room to lace and button myself into the Aunties' clothes. Rembrandt gnawed at his own back leg, a sure sign of approval.

❋

Downstairs, we met no one as we collected the tweed coat and snuck out the kitchen door. There was a large platter of bacon on the counter, and I snagged a slice for myself and one for Rembrandt. The yard was pristine again, the snow deeper still. I trudged through it up to my knees, the sodden kidskin boots tightening around my ankles, the heavy wool skirt dragging behind me like a dead thing. Invigorated by the bacon, Rembrandt shot off across the snow, hid behind the fountain, and popped out at me as I neared, snarling playfully, butting his slobbery head into my midsection. Then he took off again, toward a great stand of black trees and bushes at the far reaches of the lawn. The fountain was dry, of course, and whatever figure adorned it was bundled in a green tarp and bound with gardening twine. It could have been Saint Sebastian. It could have been a milkmaid. It looked like a corpse. The air shifted behind me, but this time I was prepared, and I turned, wrestling my frozen skirt, in time to see the owl's great eyes and tawny beak as it rushed over me. I peered in the direction from which it came. It must be nesting nearby, perhaps in the barn-cum-garage. How odd to see it in the morning; its hunger must have been immense.

As I scrutinized the house, several curtains shivered. A flash of red hair, the bulk of a bearish shadow, impeccably manicured fingertips catching the sun. I wasn't sure I warranted such attention, but maybe it meant I was on the right track. Maybe someone was nervous about what I might uncover.

❄

Rembrandt circled, running toward the black trees, then back again, wildly snapping at the air. Even for Rembrandt, this was a bit dramatic. I drew closer to the hedge and saw fluttering in its branches dozens of small white birds. This must be what had excited the dog, who continued to turn and leap in front of me. It seemed strange that the birds would have returned in the midst of such cold. I stopped to listen for their chirping, but instead heard a susurration, as if the forest beyond was hushing me. The sun came out then, and everything went white. The hissing noise grew louder as Fletcher slid into view on his cross-country skis.

I couldn't tell where he had come from because there seemed to be no break in the trees, but he had a rucksack and mirrored sunglasses and his head was bare. He laughed when he saw me wading through the snow and swooped to a halt, the tips of his skis an inch from my kneecaps. Rembrandt barked once and shied away, wheeling back to the fountain.

"Another excursion?" He gestured at the coat.

"A walk," I said, sidestepping him and trudging on.

"This way is blocked," he said, pointing to the hedge.

"You came through."

"Ahh, these woods know me. I grew up playing war in them."

"You and Dita," I said. Fletcher looked even more drawn today, as if he had spent another sleepless night.

"And Walt. He was always the hostage." His sunglasses reflected blankly at me, hiding his expression.

"But the woods won't let me pass?" I said, trying for a playfulness I couldn't quite muster.

"Exactly." Fletcher turned himself around and drew up beside me. He grasped my upper arm, hard enough to bruise. "Come back to the house, and I'll tell you stories of my misspent youth."

I yanked my arm away and at the same time tugged at the water I felt deep below the snow, pulled it to me, feeling again that strange opaque resistance at the border where the hedge was. Plumes shot from the jets of the fountain, freezing into streamers of vapor as they hit the bitter air. The sun blinked out and the clouds thickened. Fletcher didn't reach for me again, but gazed speculatively at me, his hands loose at his sides.

"You have hidden depths, Henna. Maybe the hedge would let you through after all." His sunglasses blackened with the darkening day. "Maybe we should give it a try." He grasped my arm again, in the same spot, just as hard, this time jerking me toward the trees. The distant hollow under the hawthorn bush where I'd found the dead woman beckoned. Anything could happen in the woods. Men turned wolf and back again. Girls got lost, their soft parts eaten.

"Hey." It was Walt, lumbering at a remarkable pace across the snow in my tracks, Rembrandt at his side. A grimace flashed across Fletcher's face. "Dita says it's almost lunchtime and that your dispatcher has called twice."

Fletcher smiled. "Duty calls." He V-stepped himself gracefully into the correct direction. "You'll bring Henna back safely, won't you, Walt?" he called over his shoulder as he shot off toward the house.

Walt didn't answer, but he stood staring down at me as I rubbed my arm. I hoped my strange getup wouldn't provoke any fainting spells. He scratched the ridge of Rembrandt's back and the dog moaned in pleasure, his back leg scrabbling into the snow.

"All right, then?" Walt asked as we plodded back across the lawn. He rummaged in the pocket of his anorak and came up with two white sticks—cigarettes, I thought at first, but they turned out to be peppermints, handcrafted in small batches, he told me, cold as winter on my tongue.

✽

Upstairs, I changed into a dry skirt. I was going to need a new trunk of clothes soon. Rembrandt had retreated under the bed. The lattice of water flowing from the house up to the hedge still hovered at the edge of my consciousness. It felt reassuring, this renewed awareness, and I tugged at the threads of it experimentally, as if I were the one setting a noose. I plucked the scrap of letter that Mariel had found from underneath my pillow and headed downstairs to the study. As I'd hoped, no one was around to stop me.

All the bones and hooves and antlers bristled when I entered the room. One wall was lined in bookshelves, cloth and leather-bound tomes that looked as if they hadn't been disturbed in years. There was a set of the complete works of Marlowe and a number of ancient-looking books on ornithology. A decrepit set of encyclopedias, covered in crimson, tempted me, but I passed them by to scan the shelves for diaries or logbooks, something from the ghost expedition. There were years of bound records from the village preservation board and a number of beautifully illustrated atlases. After tipping forward each of a small section of unmarked green folios that turned out to be self-published poetry, seemingly by long-dead ancestors, I shoved the books back into their places and wiped my hands on the Aunties' skirt, exasperated. So far, all I'd discovered was a lot of dust.

I dragged a chair over so I could examine the top left corner of the shelves, banking on the theory that the most interesting items would be in the most inaccessible location. I teetered on the arms of the chair, feet ungainly wide, and chinned myself up to peer into the darkest space at the top, hoping the solid old shelves would hold. A row of black ledgers made my pulse thump. They were marked with decades, starting in the early 1800s. I pulled down the one from the 1850s, and it crackled in my grip as I retreated to the desk to investigate.

Inside, the pages were divided into columns of scrolling hand-writing: lists of dates and numbers and looping phrases. *Crushed mistletoe* and *velvet musk of elk in spring* and *running water over fallen leaves.* It took me a minute, but then I realized it was another snow almanac, like the page I'd found in the library and tucked away in my doctor's bag. I flipped through the entries and eyed the dozen or so ledgers that remained on the shelf. They spanned at least 150 years, more than one man's lifetime. Perhaps it was a family pursuit, hand-ed down like the self-published poetry, another example of the fri-volity of the rich. I ascended my precarious perch again and yanked down the 1840s volume also, noting as I did that the last book was labeled 1960s. Perhaps the practice had ended then, or had begun to be recorded in some other form. I wondered if Fletcher kept a file of such descriptions on his laptop or his phone. If I was reading these correctly as perceptions of the snow on various dates, this winter had given him a lot to work with.

Seated at the desk again, I squared the two ledgers in front of me and placed the scrap of letter next to them like a talisman. *Trust you to take the greatest care* and *necessarily secret.* I remembered the same handwriting spelling *Time has come to take more decisive action* and *Hope I can rely upon your discretion and loyalty* on the fragments that were still tucked in my doctor's bag, out in my car. I turned to the last third of the 1840s ledger—columns and columns of de-scriptions, but nothing that stood out. Back in the 1850s ledger, I had to count forward to mark off the years, since the entries only marked the month and day. Only the winter months were noted, as one would expect. Most years leaped from April to October in the course of a line.

1855, the date on the letter—the year after the disastrous news from the John Rae expedition, citing Inuit reports of cooking pots and suspicious bones, along with items the Inuit had found belonging to officers from Franklin's ships, including Franklin's own gold Royal Hanoverian Guelphic Order badge, which he was never without. Franklin's name wasn't cleared until 1859, when Jane Franklin bought a ship and hired Francis Leopold McClintock to go into the ice searching for clues of his death.

I counted to January of 1855 and began reading more closely. If there had been an expedition commissioned by Jane Franklin, headed up by Fletcher's ancestor, it wouldn't have started before April or May. I trailed my finger down the browned handwriting. And there it was, May 23: *Tallow and chicken broth, granular fog driving us toward shore, kerosene and gunpowder.* June 2: *Beluga whistles puncturing pack ice, tang of blubber and blooming flesh of stranded calf, ache in the back of the throat.* June 17: *Cannonball sun skating over lichen dust, blazing ice, gold and blood and fire pooling north.* And so forth, all through the summer of that year. In the margin of one of the pages was a rough sketch of a ship, deep-chested, washed in blue watercolor, *The Champion* emblazoned on its bow. I stuck the letter fragment between the pages to mark that spot and thumbed forward to the next summer and the next. Nothing. It was back to a digest of October to April dates.

It seemed to be proof an expedition had occurred, but didn't shed light on why it was kept secret, why it didn't appear in any of the official records. In any case, I wanted a transcript of the obscure descriptions and tried the desk drawers for paper and a pen. Locked tight. Tucked into a narrow cubby on the side of the desk, I found a blank sheet thick as vellum that seemed made of some sort of hide. Recoiling, I shoved it back into its slot and left the study in search of something more modern. The door snicked closed behind me like an eye winking shut.

❄

The snow almanacs charmed me. Such a transient pursuit. Even the hydrologists I'd trained with hadn't been quite so obsessive. It was true that in graduate school, drunk on sloe gin and too many hours of dowsing, we'd talk about the textures of water, would rattle off elegies for wrung-dry aquifers, but there was nothing approaching this level of fancy. And to have kept such a continuous record, a diary that spanned generations. I imagined Fletcher's ancestors, hunting new snowfall, taking its measurements via bare skin, translating it into the least scientific of descriptions, no mention of amounts or rate of precipitation, merely scrawled lines of syllables, poetry unmoored.

❄

In the kitchen, I found a delightfully utilitarian memo pad and ballpoint. There still didn't seem to be anyone around, and I wondered if I had missed lunch or if Dita had decided it wasn't worth the trouble. I gathered provisions, just in case—an orange, a chunk of lamb on a roll, a tablet of chocolate wrapped in yellowed waxed paper stamped MEXICO.

As I went back down the dim hallway toward the study, I saw a large form disappearing into the doorway that led to the glassed passageway. It was pure impulse to follow him, to slip into the conservatory behind him, where I was hit with a wave of warmth and scent of jasmine. Inside that liquid space, all my muscles softened. Layer upon layer of green, leaves translucent in the light, vines thick as my wrists climbing the walls. I waited for the butterflies, but none appeared. Instead a cloud of gnats drifted by, in formation, funnel-shaped, then tetrahedral. Their mechanical whine was almost imperceptible. I was leaning forward, watching their retreat, when I heard a shuffling and a prolonged clearing of a throat.

"Walt?" I ventured, and he materialized from behind a vigorous shaking palm tree.

"Didn't want to startle you," he said. He waited for me to sit, then followed, the bench creaking a bit with his solid bulk. He was dressed in a furry brown sweater with his pea coat flung over one arm, and his beard was characteristically unruly. A navy stocking cap made him look like a lumberjack or a deep sea fisherman washed up onto strange shores. "Best place in the house, isn't it?"

"It's lovely. Do you wish you lived here?" I proffered the orange, and he took it tentatively, careful not to touch my hand.

"Not my side of the family."

"I thought you and Fletcher were cousins."

"Yes, but this house comes from his mother's side, and it's our fathers that were brothers. My house is the ancestral estate, such as it is, from that side, up in the old factory town." Walt took a mother-of-pearl penknife from his pocket and nicked the curve of the orange.

"But there are gloves painted on the ceiling of my bathroom."

"My uncle was a prankster. Did what he could to leave his mark on this place." The orange peel was spiraling off in a delicate twist, Walt's hands moving steadily as he looked out the glass wall before us.

"Did he die a long time ago?"

"Truck slid off the ravine, ended up headfirst in the river at the bottom. He'd been drinking. Fletcher's first year on the job, and he had to do the recovery."

I remembered Eleanor lauding the ravine's value as a moat. "That must have been awful for him."

"Hard to tell with Fletcher." Walt handed me the peel, an unbroken strand of color. "I'm headed into a couple of other villages today to make some deliveries. Want to join me?"

"But the snow," I said.

"I've dug out my truck. The main road should be clear soon." He put away his knife and split the orange down the middle. A mist of juice perfumed the air between us.

We sat in comfortable silence, each of us eating our sections of orange as they turned jewel-like in the intermittent sunlight. It was tempting to say yes and go with this big reassuring man, to get away from this house with all of its secrets. But then I remembered the ledgers and the scrap of letter still on the desk in the study and the body of the dead woman, skin frosted over, hand outstretched to me.

"I can't," I said, with real regret. "I have things I'm working on here." I trailed off, realizing how odd that must sound.

Walt leaned toward me, planting his hands palms up on the bench between us, as if in supplication. "Henna," he said, looking into my eyes, sincere as a priest or a doctor, "is there something you want to tell me?"

Again, I was tempted by his firm bulk, the safe harbor of him, but I simply put one of my hands atop his and said, "It has to do with a research question that has come up—a puzzle I'm working out."

The air buzzed with gnats and motes of dust gilded by the sun breaking through the clouds.

"It's just, you know, they have their own way of doing things here and are best left to themselves." Walt extricated his hands from mine, not looking at me as he got up and shrugged into his coat.

"Do you still have the salt?" I asked, as he was turning away.

Walt looked back at that, clearly confused.

"In your pocket, from the coffee shop?"

He reached into his pocket and came up with a trickle of salt, which he spilled into my upraised palm.

"Remember, it's good luck for travelers," I said, smiling at him.

Walt laughed, a happy guffaw. "You're making that up."

"Never," I said, and he laughed again, touched his hand to my shoulder as if we were indeed traveling companions.

"Then I've got luck for centuries, out in the back of my pickup, ready to be parceled out for the right price." He laughed a third time, and his hand drifted up to the side of my face. His fingers were scented with sweet orange. The orchids leaned toward us in their glass cloches, drawn by the quickening of my blood.

❄

The door at the other end of the atrium, the locked door, swung open with a tremendous squeal and Fletcher stepped through. His appearance was a shock; I thought he'd gone to the station. When he caught sight of us, he stopped, shoved his thumbs in his waistband, and rocked back on his heels. "What a pretty picture you two make. Having a picnic?"

"Actually, I was headed out." Walt said, pulling his hand away from me and tugging his stocking cap firmly down over his brow. "Just checking to see if Henna wanted to come with me today."

"Why would she want to do that?" Fletcher moved forward and leaned into my side. He threw off heat like a horse that has been running hard. "Be rather boring, wouldn't it, accompanying you on your rounds?" I thought of the games he and Dita used to play with Walt in the woods. Walt looked like he was a hostage all over again.

Sun flooded the passageway, making it glow green. I lifted my face to the light. "I'm okay here," I said, stepping into the pool of fear that was opening in me. I still had threads to unravel. And then there was my trick with the fountain that morning—more water than I'd been able to pull in ages. Fletcher's growing sharpness was calling an answering edge in me, and I held my dowsing between us like a knife.

Walt huffed out a breath and turned to go.

"Safe travels, cousin." Fletcher's hand landed hard on my shoulder, holding me down, and I wondered how much he had overhead.

By the time the door closed behind Walt, Fletcher had found my packet of food and was feeding me strips of the lamb that he tore apart efficiently. He licked one finger and dipped it into the salt in my palm to taste it, saying, "Salt or sugar, Henna? With you I never know." I lifted my mouth to his so he could get a better sense and didn't wince when he drew blood.

While he was distracted, I tipped the rest of the salt into the top of my boot, saving a little luck for later. The chocolate we split down the middle, but either it had turned bitter or had begun that way.

❄

After lunch, Fletcher roared off on Plover's snowmobile, which he said he had used to take him home the night before with a make-shift sledge. Once he was gone, I hurried through the house to the study, clutching the memo pad I'd taken from the kitchen, eager to get back to the snow almanac. There was still no sign of Dita, and I wondered when she did her cleaning.

I thrust open the door of the study and found Eleanor at the desk, scratching away in a brown leather-covered journal with an antique fountain pen. She sat ramrod straight and didn't budge an inch when I burst into the room, merely lifting her eyes to glance at me over the tops of her reading glasses. She was dressed in immaculate ivory again, from her trim suit to her hose to her shoes. The desktop was clear of volumes except for her journal, no sign of the snow almanacs or the scrap of letter.

"Yes?" she raised her eyebrows.

"I didn't mean to disturb you." I felt my breath coming faster, wondering what excuse I could give for coming in here. Clearly, she had found the ledgers and the letter fragment. She must know I had left them there. Or maybe it was Dita who had found them, straightening up while I was in the passageway with Fletcher. "I was just looking for something to read."

"Last week's paper is on the table in the foyer."

"I was thinking of a novel." I wandered toward the bookshelves, trying to see whether the ledgers had been replaced. There seemed to still be a black gap in the row.

"Oh." She looked round at the deer hooves littering the desk. "I never read fiction."

We seemed to be at an impasse, but I couldn't leave without trying to figure out if she had been the one to find the snow almanacs on the desk. If she had, perhaps I could make up an explanation about doing research for an encyclopedia entry, probe whether she had seen the scrap of letter, find out what she knew about Jane Franklin and the expedition. I came closer, trying discreetly to see if any of the drawers were ajar. Maybe she had stashed the ledgers in one of them. Everything was just as it had been, shut tight. Stalling, I picked up one of the photo frames from the corner of the desk and rubbed my thumb over the paled-out faces. "Are these your family photos or your husband's?" I asked her.

"Mine, of course. Everything in this house is from my side. They were the leading family in this area, generations of honorable men and women working for the greater good. I've been careful to preserve as much of their legacy as possible." She leaned forward to pull the frame from me. "Some things can't be saved," she rubbed her own finger over the blank faces, "but with work, most can be protected. Or restored."

Eleanor drew herself abruptly, impossibly, straighter and said, "I owe you an apology for Vedius's behavior last night." I looked blankly at the flaps of ostrich skin hanging from the wall behind her. "Plover provoked him, of course, but his training should have held."

Ah, yes, the bird. I waved my hands as if to brush away her words. "It was Walt who was injured."

There was a pause as we both contemplated the wealth of dismembered parts surrounding us.

"He seems like a very fine bird," I offered.

"He is. And Plover is a fool. His idiotic venture. What a waste of resources. And he imagines people will flock to him." Her mouth twisted in dismay.

"Perhaps they will. We like to remember how things used to be."

Eleanor shook her head once, impatiently. "No. If there was a science to it, maybe. If people could go to him to study, to advance their knowledge, then there would be a value to it. But with him, it is all spectacle."

I didn't know why I was defending Plover and his odd museum, but I felt compelled to insist, "It's still a starting point."

"It is a false start that will lead to a bad end. One must be precise, must act out of a love for the subject if one is to embark upon a scientific pursuit. It is why I keep these records of the birds, what they've eaten, how they've slept, when they molt." She tapped the pen against the journal. "I wish I could show you something that would prove my point. It is the work of generations of my family: a collection of snow samples from this area, some of the vials dating back nearly two centuries, meticulously catalogued, a gift for future generations."

I flinched at the mention of an actual snow collection to go along with the almanacs. Eleanor peered at me, as if challenging me to confess. Perhaps I should ask about the ledgers after all. She must have been the one to find them, and now she was just baiting me. The light shifted in the room, and her eyes were blank coins glaring at me. I knew then how easily she would have killed that woman if she felt her family was threatened, if the woman had come bearing a letter that seemed to reveal some unsavory episode, a secret Eleanor's ancestors had promised to keep. I felt the chill go right through me, as if exhaled from the snow almanacs themselves.

"I'd love to see it," I said, edging toward the door.

Eleanor spoke softly. "But I can't show it to you. He keeps it locked now, all these weeks, ever since the last time Plover was here.

That man carries bad luck with him." I wondered if she was talking about the room of freezers, if perhaps they constituted the collection, but couldn't remember whether the door had been locked or merely latched. She said without inflection, "He is an abomination and my son too lenient. Franklin's job has made him soft, made him forget one must protect one's own above all others." Eleanor's unfocused eyes scared me more than anything else in this long winter. The bones in the room seemed to be exuding a faint scent of decay. "And since that night, he hasn't let me in."

I waited for her to continue, but she simply stared out the window at the white expanse of the yard and the distant hedge. The nib of her pen pressed so hard into the journal that I was afraid it would snap. She didn't seem to notice the blot of ink spreading across the paper, and she didn't move as I backed from the room, into the hull of the house.

VANISHING POINT

LWAYS, SO MUCH TO DO. Letters to write, visits to be made, trips to arrange, a stepdaughter to be put off. The plans for the statue in Waterloo Place were grand, but the monument needed to be pushed back eighteen inches for the best aspect. Her niece, Sophy, had measured, on hands and knees, while Jane directed. India was calling to her; she had not climbed the stairs of Qutb-Minar on her last visit, and she hated to miss an elevation. The dean of Westminster had not replied to her since she had refused the compliment of a window rather than a bust in Franklin's honor.

She was seventy-eight and not one bit tired. Didn't she get up each morning to cover every inch of her body, but for her face, in silk and tweed and leather ? Didn't children still sing her lament in the streets? Somewhere, her husband waited. This, she knew. She'd build him up again, in marble and verse, in proclamations, in missives to and from the next generation of explorers. Her memories of him were transient things: the cream he poured on his toast, his fleshy earlobes, the clack of his walking stick—details that must be subsumed into a cenotaph that would outlive both of them.

One day, she would rest; she would sit in the tub, daydreaming of gothic terrors as she used to. One day, she might remember the course of her life as a choice instead of a trap. But for now, she must follow where the roads ran, and where there were no roads, she must forge them.

CHAPTER FIFTEEN

*T*HE DRESS WAS A WRECK. I'd sewn up the bodice to the best of my ability, which meant clumps of violet thread zigzagged across my chest as if an inept autopsy had been performed. The steadiness of my hands hadn't been improved by my increasing certainty that Eleanor had killed that woman. She said the snow collection had been off limits *since that night* and had been furious when Plover reappeared. So the snow collection must be something separate from the freezers, which Fletcher seemingly had no compunction about showing me. I thought about the locked door at the end of the glassed passageway and wondered again what lay behind it.

By now, like any grief-stricken, Arctic-obsessed amateur sleuth, I had a theory. The woman must have made her way to the house with evidence of the secret expedition, though it was incomprehensible to me why that would stoke Eleanor's protective instincts to such an extreme. Regardless, I imagined Plover had been here with Eleanor. Why else would he have been so horrified when I'd told him where I was staying? Maybe Fletcher had been out patrolling that night. Maybe he didn't realize that his mother had been the one to—what? Kill the woman and dump her body? Improbable—anyway, the coroner had said she died of exposure. I could, however, imagine Eleanor driving the woman out into the snow, from some twisted desire to preserve the family legacy.

I needed to talk to Fletcher, gauge how much he knew. He'd seemed so shaken when he'd told me about the woman's identity and the letter she bore; it seemed impossible that he had witnessed what occurred. More likely, he had found out about it afterward and was covering for his mother. It was possible even Fletcher wasn't sure what had happened that night in his house. Perhaps his recent scare tactics were meant to deter me from alerting Eleanor to my suspicions, to keep me safe. Or perhaps I was blinded by a spot of canoodling, oldest trick in the book.

The boots had shrunken from repeated exposure to the snow and cut off the circulation to my feet. I was tempted to go barefoot like Dita, but, feeling the lucky salt rolling against my right sole, resisted my bohemian impulses, cinched the corset tighter, jabbed my head with the hairpins, and even screwed on a pair of earrings I'd unearthed from the bottom of the trunk. The paste had gone cloudy with age, moonstones now instead of diamonds, good for fortune telling.

❋

I looked like a caricature of one of the stern ancestors on the walls that I passed going downstairs. I felt the Aunties chuckling deep underground. The dining room table was naked. I poked my head into the kitchen and found a frazzled-looking Dita, clad in a diaphanous skirt made of layers of scarves, along with a corset of her own, but pink sateen and studded. Over this, a tattered brown cardigan that could have been one of Walt's, and in her ears twenty silver spikes, her cartilage weighed down. I hadn't noticed the holes before. She was ladling tomato soup out of a pot on the stove and called over her shoulder, "Come help me carry these." I grabbed two bowls, and she started as I came into view. "I thought you were Fletcher," she said, in a tone of disapproval.

"Here I am." He strolled into the kitchen, palms upturned. "Mother isn't feeling well. She wants her dinner upstairs." I felt a great surge

of relief and wondered when I could get him alone to talk about my
suspicions, considered what proof I could offer him.

"I'll take her some when we're finished," Dita said and thrust a
bowl of rolls into his hands.

We arranged ourselves around the table, with as much space between us as possible. The meal was a silent affair. The soup tasted of
metal. The rolls were stones Dita had dug from the backyard. The
candles stayed unlit. Rembrandt wandered in halfway through, the
first time he had ventured out of the bedroom on his own. Dita
whistled in exasperation, lured him into the kitchen with a roll, and
shut the door behind him.

"That should hold him a while." Fletcher laughed.

"Fuck off," Dita said and whipped her hair over her shoulder.

"Charming," Fletcher said, sipping at his soup.

"I'm sorry, but we're running low on supplies," Dita retorted.
"Walt called to say he's staying overnight with some fellow farmer. I
thought our guest would have gone by now and that you would be at
the station." She said *our guest* with a throat full of acid.

"Slow night," Fletcher said, ignoring her comment about me. I
gnawed my roll in silence.

"How long are you planning to stay, Henna?" Dita flung her
chin toward me.

"Enough." Fletcher put down his spoon.

"It's just that we aren't used to having company. The last one
didn't stay so long." Her ear spikes bristled.

Fletcher reached across the table to grab her wrist, spilling the
soup she was spooning up. "Go up to Mother now. She'll be wondering about her dinner."

Dita stared at him for a moment, then wrested her arm away
and pushed back her chair with a clatter. "You just won't listen to
sense, will you?" she shot over her shoulder as she slammed into the
kitchen. It was unclear whom she was asking.

The last one. It had to be the dead woman. So Fletcher knew she'd been at the house. Maybe I shouldn't go to him after all. It was clear mother and son doted on each other. Maybe I should pack up Rembrandt and go to the authorities. It wasn't what you'd hope from a gothic heroine, but it was sensible. Except that as far as I knew, Fletcher was the authority for miles around.

I would gather up what evidence I could and head out in the light of morning to another village, find another police chief to tell my story to, lay it at someone else's feet. Maybe the ledgers had been replaced. Maybe the scrap of letter was still inside the 1850s one, marking the only record I'd found of the secret expedition that seemed to be at the heart of this. Maybe the snow collection, if I could find it, would be the key. Or perhaps I'd wander around the house until I found a secret tunnel to a monastery filled with murderous monks, or else Fletcher's Drummond ancestor would speak to me through a portrait, send some ancient armor after me, torment me into a tumble down the cellar steps. There were so many possibilities for a woman in my position.

"Don't mind her. She has moods," Fletcher said, reaching for my hand. His thumb was sandpaper across my knuckles. "But she's right that I need to go check on things in town."

"So the roads really are clear now, all the way up to the house?" I asked.

"Yes, but don't get any ideas." He pulled my hand toward him and bit my index finger, none too lightly. He looked at me speculatively, and I held my breath, wondering if Eleanor had told him about the snow almanacs and the new scrap of letter. "I'll only be gone a couple of hours. I'll tell you a bedtime story when I get back." His teeth flashed at me, and the sense of dread welling in me crested.

Dita thumped back through the kitchen door, breaking the spell. I caught a glimpse of Rembrandt curled under the table in there, happily investigating himself. Fletcher dropped my hand, shot to his feet, and said, "I'm off."

He and Dita left the dining room together. I watched the soup congeal for a while before I carried the bowls into the kitchen and washed them in the sink. The cloud of suds was so ordinary, I almost felt I was at home for a moment: the crash of surf on the rocks, the brackish smell of wetsuits drying on the deck rails. And then a cry came from the woods, something hunting, and I remembered the cold I had chosen.

I threw Rembrandt another roll. Then I left him there and slipped back into the dark maze of the house, pulled toward the lodestone of that locked door.

❄

At night, the glass passageway was not so welcoming. I had a candle and a full moon washing in through the windows. I wondered where the hell Fletcher kept his flashlights. The orchids glowed. At first, I thought the tops of their bell jars were frosted over, but then realized they were crusted with moths that flickered as I walked by. The sky was cloudless and yet the snow was coming down, hard little chips of stars pelting the glass. The door was identical to the one at the other end, but the knob would not turn.

I took a pair of hairpins from my head and wiggled them in the lock experimentally. They bent at once. Luckily, I had two dozen more pricking my scalp. The third pair took. I felt one catch, and then the whole mechanism turned, heavy as a footfall, solid as a hand on my shoulder. Gooseflesh rose on my arms. The candle guttered but stayed lit, and the door swung open into a darker dark.

❄

Before me was a pathway of rooms and hallways, each with a light switch conveniently at hand as I came through the doors. It was the mirror of the other wing of the house, and I circled it slowly, feeling nostalgic for bird droppings and Dita's cooking. These rooms were empty, pristine, free of dust or furniture or clues. No revelations or torture chambers awaited after all. And then, where the cellar door was in the other wing, I found another lock. Three more sets of hairpins and I was in.

Instead of stairs heading down, there was just an empty room. Or not quite empty. This room held a large cabinet, glass-fronted, that glimmered in the light from the hall. There was no switch, so I held my candle close to peer at it. The cabinet doors swung open soundlessly at my touch. Inside were dozens of drawers, made of polished black wood.

I opened one drawer and reached in. My hand met skin. I drew out a pair of gloves, soft as petals. Another drawer, another pair, all softer than the last. The final drawer held nothing, but as I pulled it fully open, a grinding sound came from behind me, and I turned in time to see the wall split, a panel slide open, and a glowing aperture appear.

❋

I entered, of course. How could I resist a secret passage when I'd wished so hard for one? Five steps down and I was in the treasure room. Sconces glowed softly. The walls were lined with bookshelves filled with ivory boxes and brass instruments, and rows of what looked like ships' logs and old journals. To my left was a stack of ancient trunks, salt-stained and reeking of the ocean. Their brass fittings were green, their sides bowed. A glass case beside them held an old jacket, fur-trimmed, moth-eaten, shaped into the form of a stocky man. The case was stacked with dented rusty food tins and battered pewter mugs and what looked like a chess set crudely carved from bone. Dangling in front of the case was a model of a ship: small and bulky, polished oak, painted cobalt below the waterline, deep-chested as a bull. *The Champion* emblazoned on its bow. My breath quickened at the sight. These had to be the trappings of the secret expedition.

As I stepped closer to investigate, an overhead fixture clicked on and cast a circle of light into the center of the room, illuminating a waist-high table, enormous and square. It was a map of sorts, and as I drew near, I saw it was the Arctic sculpted in wood, ice floes and all. Two ships stood proud, black bodies, with a yellow stripe banding each, *Erebus* and *Terror* painted on their sides. They were in full sail, penned by ice. Across the great white expense, landmarks were marked in gold calligraphy—Boothey Peninsula, Rae Strait, King William Island.

I reached out and touched the tip of one of the ships' masts. A whirring started up, and tiny metal men poured onto deck. They furled the sails, packed the sledges, hacked at the ice with pickaxes. A group of three men took off across the ice with rifles and a spear and came back with a wooden seal, head lolling, painted wounds. Some of the men fell to the decks of the ships and stopped moving. At first their comrades picked them up and buried them in the snow. And then the *Erebus* drifted off and stuck again, and after that, when the men fell, the others didn't seem to notice.

Finally all of the remaining men took to the ice, dragging wooden rowboats behind them, filled with miniscule pots and pans, bibles, guns, packets labeled chocolate and tobacco. Leading them was a portly figure, rosy-lipped, a clutch of cross-shaped medals on his uniform jacket. The ships listed behind them, sinking into the ice. The metal men walked on. Some fell over; some went to their knees for a bit and then stood. The leader seemed to be yelling orders, though of course, no sound emerged. And then the figures sped up, more and more falling, the rowboats stuck in the snow, the remaining circle of men setting on the fallen, raising their axes, gathered by a fire, glass shards that glowed to illuminate the little men hungrily stripping the meat from the bones.

I watched until the last man had tipped over onto the wooden ice and shuddered into stillness. Then I lifted him up and shook him. Something rattled inside. At the edge of the map, a narwhal's tusk protruded and retreated. Miniature blocks of ice climbed up over the ships and hid them from view, and the whole thing ground to a halt with a clamor of crushing gears.

❄

The silence was broken by the sound of clapping behind me on the stairs. I whirled as fast as my corset would allow. Dita stood there, hair wild, lipstick chewed off. She'd lost her sweater, and her bare shoulders gleamed like marble. "You've found it," she crowed.

I backed away from her, ramming a hip into the table. She advanced toward me carefully, as if approaching a strange animal.

"You know what it means, right? You've figured out the secret?" She gestured to the fallen figurines. "For so long now, it has been up to Fletcher's family to keep it all hidden. She entrusted them with it, and nobody ever figured it out."

"Who entrusted them with it?" I asked, feeling behind me for something I could use as a weapon if it came to that.

Dita kept coming, slowly. Her lips were worms. "Don't play stupid. Lady Jane, of course. The great patroness, she who traded in gold and feathers—the benefactress for whom Fletcher is named."

My mind flashed on the portrait of Jane from her biography: clever eyes, poof of curls, half smirk, a thousand letters written on her husband's behalf. The secret expedition she had commissioned from Drummond, the ledger with the qualities of Arctic snow, lovingly recorded, but no other sign outside this room.

Dita picked up a tiny metal thighbone, flayed of flesh. "You see now?"

"But people know about the cannibalism. Even at the time, there were rumors. But Sir John had already died, was honorably buried by the time things got that bad."

Dita tapped the little man with the cross medals, sitting upright at the fire. "Was he?"

"There was proof—the note found by McClintock on King William Island. Franklin died well before the men set off, starving." I wasn't sure why I was reviewing nineteenth-century history with Dita at this moment, especially as she began to move toward me again, smiling beatifically.

"See, you know all about it," Dita said, drawing close enough to kiss. "Pity. Now you'll disappear and things will go back to how they ought."

"But I don't know," I protested. "None of that is secret."

Dita leaned in, her forehead almost touching mine. One of the silver spikes trembled where it had nearly been torn out, and blood pooled in the cup of her ear. I wondered who had done it, what drama was being played out in the main house while I hunted out secret passageways and hidden artifacts. I cursed myself for my blindness in assuming it had been Eleanor, or Eleanor alone, who'd caused the woman's death. My hands scrabbled behind me and lit upon something round that turned out to be a doorknob, which I wrenched at unsuccessfully.

Dita rushed at me and clawed my cheek. I fought to get the door open, but it opened inward and we were pressed against it. Dita was a feral creature, roaring and pounding at me, and she didn't notice Fletcher behind her until he tore her weight off of me and threw her back, toward the room with the cabinet of gloves.

❄

Years later, this was the moment that would haunt my dreams. Fletcher walking softly toward me, Dita's body crumpled behind him, my hand slipping ineffectually on the door knob—and something else at my back, a swelling, as if we were in the deep and the ocean was trying to break through.

❄

Fletcher closed on me. He touched the bloody marks on my cheek gently and said, "I'm glad you know, Henna. I didn't like keeping things from you."

"I don't know," I repeated, trying to breathe against the force of the wave building around me.

"Charles Drummond. My great-great-grandfather." Fletcher sounded amused, as if tickled by my denseness. He gestured at the hollow coat in the case, the hanging ship, the stained trunks. "His expedition, his sacred favor to Lady Jane. He styled himself her champion. He added that postscript to the note, the one reporting Sir John's death. The irony is, he made a great find—the cache with its document—and didn't even get to claim it. Instead, he created a false history to be found by someone else, and then had to keep the real one hidden, locked away here in this house where only his family could appreciate it."

His hand was at my throat now. It may have been better for me to have kept silent then, but I'd never been able to resist an unraveling. And his hand was light on me.

"How does Lady Jane come into it? Why keep the expedition secret?"

"She lost faith, Henna. The family story is that a ghost girl told her where they'd find the cache, gave her explicit instructions, but no one was bringing back the evidence she needed. So she gave up on her husband and tended to his shell instead." His words were whispered, as if we were lovers exchanging vows.

I stared at him in horror. I hadn't misheard—he really was saying that Lady Jane had commissioned his ancestor to exonerate her husband with a fabricated log. If true, it would be a rip in history that would bleed into the hundreds of accounts written about the most famous Arctic voyage.

I swallowed hard, and Fletcher's fingers tightened on me and then dropped. He pulled me to his chest and spoke into my hair. "And the shell holds. Even with that woman bringing her *discovery* here, her *shocking conspiracy*. She thought we would be *interested*. She underestimated our interest, didn't she?"

Fletcher let me go to reach behind me. The doorknob turned easily under his touch.

❋

I could do nothing but step into that dark room, Fletcher following. My eyes adjusted to the small space that was limned with moonlight from a many-paned door at the end.

"The real treasure," Fletcher said, advancing at my side. The room was narrow, lined with glass cases filled with hundreds of vials that sloshed as I entered. I could just make out a swarm of dates and places scrawled across their labels. The containers were of all shapes and sizes—flasks and test tubes, perfume bottles, pickle jars, ampoules stoppered with cork and wax and metal. The snow collection.

The melted snow exuded a scent. It was the smell of starved blood and ocean voyages, of watered-down turpentine, rotting fruit, the fragrance of a thousand kisses gone astray, the dried remains of small animals in the forest, the salt of an oyster's milk. And something else, some newer scent overlaying all the others. I couldn't get away from it fast enough. I stepped forward to press my palms against the cold panes of the door to the outside.

Fletcher was at my shoulder, speaking into my ear. "You don't want to run, Henna. That's what she did, and it didn't work out well."

Of course the dead woman had been in this room. It was her tears I smelled.

❋

I should have fled then, but I was drowning in the decades of melted snow. It was so heavy, I couldn't catch my breath. Fletcher turned me to him, held my face in his hands, careful with the scratches Dita had left there.

"I tried to save her, but she came here uninvited, and Mother guards our legacy so jealously. She would have vanished her completely if not for Plover's presence. She's not very happy with you right now either. It was all I could do to convince her to let me be the one to deal with you, and even then, Dita thought to take matters into her own hands."

"The woman came here with Plover?" My thoughts were sodden, moving slowly through the information. Stupid woman, stumbling across a secret that was well over a century old and thinking it needed to be told. I felt a stab of recognition.

Fletcher stroked my face, the scratches aching at his touch. "No. Ill luck, that. Plover was already here that night, angling for the glaciers. I wasn't planning to sell them, but what choice did I have once he'd seen the woman at my house? In exchange, he agreed not to go into the village; he has no control over his tongue." He sounded like we were having tea, but his hand was smeared now with my blood.

"And you, dear Henna—well, I won't call that bad luck, though I didn't think the woman would make it so far when I gave her the choice to run. She was quick, managed to take the letter with her and get through the hedge before I could follow. I figured the weather would take care of her, since I'd beguiled her down here without her coat or shoes."

I closed my mind to what form this beguilement might have taken, remembering the bitter taste of chocolate. Fletcher grasped my face and my hands came up to dig at his wrists. "You have to see I gave her a fighting chance. Mother would not have been so merciful."

Idly, I wondered how Eleanor would have done it. Portioned her to feed the birds? But really, I should have known it was Fletcher, always popping up, first on the scene, handing out grimly amused warnings.

I did not shy away when he lowered his mouth to mine. I had no room to move. Around us, the glass jars began to tremble.

He spoke so low, it was as if I were intuiting the words from the motion of his lips. "Stay with us, Henna. You and I would suit." His grip was hard on my jaw. The snow grew heavier. It would bury us if it could. "You have nothing else, no one to call your own. Here, you could have all of this."

Fletcher stepped back then, to gesture at the crowded walls. My fingertips tingled as my blood surged outward. In the room behind him, Dita made wet gasping sounds, as if choking.

As he turned to look at her, the vials rattled violently and then exploded in a maelstrom of glass. The melted snow flooded the room, more water than seemed possible. Fletcher staggered and was swept away from me, the mingled odors rising up between us like a hundred spirits, fogging my vision. I wrestled the door open and flew out into the icy yard.

❄

My feet were hooves in their hardened boots. I panted as I ran, drawing the cold air into my dry lungs. It felt as if all the liquid of my body was still trapped in that narrow room.

Halfway across the lawn, I could hear Fletcher behind me, but when I turned to see, it wasn't he who followed, but rather a flock of large dark birds, streaming from an upstairs window, at which Eleanor stood, hair gleaming. The birds were silent except for the terrible sound of their wings beating in one great mass as they drew closer. I forced myself to run faster.

There was the crash of glass breaking and Rembrandt's yowl. I risked a backward glance to see him pelting toward me from the direction of the conservatory. In the moonlight, he was an unlikely savior, his ears flying and great paws flinging snow.

Something sharp raked my back. It felt as if my body was unfurling, a great blossom of pain rushing out behind me. And then a furious scream and the sound of rending, panicked croaks filling the air like rioting winds. I was at the hedge, so I turned to look. The owl had come down amidst the flock and was tearing it left and right, swooping in great arcs, wings like sails in the night.

❄

I turned to the black branches, determined to find a path through them, and was surprised to see the pale birds from earlier in the day still perched there, fluttering. I raised my hand to one of them and found they were not birds at all but scraps of paper. This had to be the rest of the letter the dead woman had borne, shredded on the thorns of the hedge. I grabbed for them. Curiosity, that stubborn flail. But the paper was blank. As was the next scrap, and the next. And then Fletcher was beside me, and one of his hands trapped my wrists while the other pressed into the flower of pain on my back where the skin was torn.

"Henna, what will I do with you?" He was still amused, but just. "Your house burning down was a mistake. All along, I only meant to scare you away from asking questions, so I could keep you for myself, but I think we've gone beyond that now." He pulled me up against him, pressed me close with a hand that felt as if it was burrowing into my spine. His teeth were very white. "Head start?" he asked, and I felt my wrists crack in his grasp.

❄

But I didn't need my hands to dowse. I felt for that strange barrier beneath the hedge, and it spewed up, black poison spilling onto the snow—the ink that had washed from the letter, a mourning border enclosing the house. As the shadow seeped toward us, Fletcher raised his face from mine. He released my hands and stumbled back as the black pooled at his feet.

Misdirection had always been my strength, but my aim was pretty good too. I flung the pins from my hair as fast as I could pull them. Fletcher yelled, covering his eyes, and Rembrandt slammed into him, glittering with shards from the kitchen window, decaying old fangs bared. He caught Fletcher's shoulder in his mouth and savaged it, dragging him onto his back, but released him without hesitation when I called. The hedge opened for us, and no thorn touched us as we sped through. Behind us, Fletcher buried his face into the snow, as if it might heal him. Perhaps it would.

The branches thinned, and one final slip of paper chattered at me as I passed. Then Rembrandt and I were clear, stumbling through the woods, across fallen logs and small solid streams. We ran and ran. I was aiming for the beehives; I knew I could find my way to Mariel's from there. I reached out for the viscous lure of honey, but we must have been too far away, so we ran blindly.

I was cold as the moon by the time we broke out of the forest onto the side of the ploughed asphalt and I realized I had gone the wrong way—away from Mariel's, toward the road that wound to Fletcher's house. I could see it there, crouched on the hill above me, windows dark, as if the inhabitants were fast asleep.

❄

I kept to side of the road as I climbed the hill toward the house, despite the berm of salt and grit and slush the plow had left there. Rembrandt trudged along behind me, the adrenaline finally worn off. The winding driveway was barely plowed; we slipped and slithered our way up it until we reached the clearing in front of the house. I grabbed Rembrandt tightly by the ruff and stood in the shadow of a large pine as I scanned the façade. All dark, no movement, no rustling curtains or flicker of candlelight. It was as if I had dreamt that mad confrontation with Fletcher, as if nothing had happened at all. My car sat in its spot next to the garage, reassuringly ordinary, coated with snow. The garage doors were closed, so I couldn't see if Fletcher's truck was there. I assumed he had shot off in it to hunt me down, but I didn't want to be surprised. I crept up to the windows in the garage doors, dragging Rembrandt along with me. The moon fell toward the horizon, puncturing the clouds.

❋

The garage was empty. I let out the breath I'd been holding, then scurried across to my car, where I stayed as low as possible while knocking the snow off the windshield with my hands and forearms. My fingers were so numb they felt like sticks scraping the glass. Finally, I'd cleared a small circle. I thrust Rembrandt into the back seat. The door shutting behind him was like a gunshot, and I huddled beside the car, looking up at the house again for any sign of life. Nothing. So I bundled myself into the driver's seat and rummaged through my doctor's bag on the floor of the passenger's side.

My hands were nearly useless now, but I managed to clamp the key in my palm and wedge it into the ignition. The car stuttered to life, headlights shining weakly through the packed-on snow. The heat that barely trickled out of the vents felt like heaven. My back screamed against the seat—I was afraid to think of the damage the birds' talons had wreaked. The memory of the salt in my boot flashed into my mind, but the leather was soaked through, and the salt was undoubtedly long gone. I'd have to make my own luck, I thought, as I pressed down the accelerator, wrenched the car around the clearing, and roared down the drive between the sentinels of black pines.

❄

I realized as soon as we started down the long hill that the dangerous part of the night was just beginning. The road was slick with snow and patches of ice, and my tires spun wildly as we careened from turn to turn. The circle I'd cleared on the windshield rapidly iced over, and the wipers filmed the glass until it looked like the backside of a mirror. I knew the ravine was on my right, so I held to the left and prayed I wouldn't meet any other cars. Rembrandt whined in the backseat. I slowed to a crawl, but I no longer had control of the car; it was sliding down the curves of the hill on its own, and all I could do was try to steer. I hadn't cleared the back window, nor the sides, so there was no way to see if someone was following us. It was as if we were in a submarine, navigating by sonar.

Then, a great flash across the windshield as the lights of another vehicle struck it. I saw a dark shape looming and pulled right, clenching my palms around the quaking steering wheel. My tire caught on the embankment at the edge of the road, and for a moment, I thought we'd stay on, but then we slid sickeningly off the side and bowled down a steep slope. Sapling trunks snapped as we trundled over them, until suddenly the car listed toward the passenger side and came to halt with a thump as we hit something solid.

I was afraid to move, fearing we might dislodge whatever balance was keeping us from tumbling farther into the ravine. In the rearview mirror, I saw Rembrandt had been thrown to the floor, but he seemed to be unharmed. He was busy worrying his back leg. I considered whether I could somehow push the car back onto the road. A few minutes of the chill settling in, watching my headlights grow ever fainter, and it became clear there was nothing for it but to abandon our vessel and walk. I was so tired, I would have burrowed there, let my bones be found come spring or lost forever, but the sound of Rembrandt's methodical licking goaded me. I gathered up the doctor's bag, hoping I'd forgotten something useful like fur-lined gloves or a granola bar in it, and cautiously cracked open my door.

The car was tilted alarmingly to the right, so I had to pull myself gingerly out by the doorframe. As I looked up the slope that led to road, I saw a blaze of light on the pavement and the dark figure of a man, silhouetted, moving toward me. Every muscle in my body froze and thawed and froze again in the seconds before Walt reached me and extended his hand to pull me fully from the wreck of the car.

❅

It was a while before I was warm enough to understand that Walt had developed a fit of conscience, which prodded him from the shelter of his farmer friend's house to return and check on me. With both of us pushing, we got his truck fully back onto the road, and I'd asked him to drive us as far away from the house as possible. I must have been more desperate-looking than I thought, because he didn't argue, just took to the highway and headed north.

It took longer for me to tell him about the treasure room and the strange story of a secret expedition and how Fletcher had chased the dead woman into the woods. By the time I stopped talking, my fingers had warmed and my feet were throbbing.

Walt reached over and plucked at the scarred-over bodice of my dress. Rembrandt snuffled disapprovingly from where he was crowded at my feet. Walt handed me a bit of white he'd pulled from the silk—that last scrap of paper that had fluttered at the end of the hedge. This one had writing on it, blue ballpoint, the rounded letters spelling the name of the village and *Notre-Dame-de-Bon-Secours* with the address in Montreal. It was the note I'd found in the pink puffer jacket, and I stared at it, astonished at its reappearance. Had Fletcher been disposing of the jacket in the woods when I'd caught him coming back through the hedge that morning with his rucksack? Had the house expelled the note on its own, as protective of the past as its inhabitants? It seemed I would never know. Maybe the note had simply flocked to me like the fragments of Lady Jane's letter, drawn to me like water.

"*Notre-Dame-de-Bon-Secours*," I read aloud. "Our Lady of Good Luck, right?" I thought again of the salt melted into my boot.

"Good Help," Walt corrected. "It's a church in Montreal. They call it the Sailor's Church because it's near the docks, and men used to go there to leave offerings for safe voyages." He peered at the scrap when I held it up to him.

"How do you know?" I was glad to find my distrustfulness still intact.

"My farm isn't far from the border, and I go to Montreal a lot to source things for the restaurant." Walt reached over to pat my arm, his hand like a great paw. "Truth is, I search out good spaces. Ever since I served." He scrubbed harder at his face. "I guess it is as close as I get to praying."

We both were silent for a moment, contemplating the dark around us. Walt glanced at me.

"I shouldn't have left you there, Henna. It was wrong, but that place messes with me, brings back bad memories."

"I can see why." I placed my hand over the back of his where it rested between us. "And it wasn't all bad," I added, thinking of sharing the orange with him in the glassed passageway, the way the gnats sang for us. "The lucky salt is gone," I reported, feeling unaccountably sad over this small loss.

The cab of the truck shook with Walt's laughter. "Plenty more where that came from." He turned his hand up to clasp mine, but kept his eyes on the road as he said, "Are we going traveling, then?"

Rembrandt gave a happy grunt. The road scrolled before us like a fissure opening in the pack ice.

❉

We drove into Canada at a small border crossing, just one lane and a bored guard flicking through a binder. My doctor's bag disgorged my passport, no worse for wear. The guard seemed to know Walt, turned jocular even as he looked askance at my damp finery and disheveled hair. He asked how we met. Walt raised my hand to his lips and declared, "She was haunting me." Evidently, the guard was a romantic, because he waved us through.

I must have slept then. I don't remember anything until Walt touched my shoulder to alert me to the city, and I found myself curled against his sturdy side. In the distance, the horizon began to blush.

❉

The church of Notre-Dame-de-Bon-Secours was smaller than I'd expected: light stone, well-proportioned, with a modest steeple echoed by a slighter spire on each side. There were arched windows and the hint of angels' wings from statues set at the back of the building. We found the door unlocked even though it was still not fully light. We left Rembrandt in the running truck, preoccupied with one of Walt's work gloves he had commandeered and was pretending was a rabbit.

Inside, the church was faintly lit by a few ornate chandeliers and banks of candles against the walls. Walt surprised me by performing obeisance as we entered, holy water at the cardinal points, down on one knee, a suitor for our lady. I turned away, shy witness, and noticed a plaque of marble set into the wall next to the door listing the names of sponsors for a renovation of the chapel in 1858. Charles Drummond was listed second. This was why the woman had the church's name with her. She must have come across the connection in her research into Fletcher's ancestor. Upon his safe return from the secret expedition, Drummond had given to the church so generously he was immortalized in its walls.

Walt scuffed his feet and slipped a pamphlet from a stack. I turned back and was struck by the chapel in its entirety. Suspended from the ceiling were gorgeously detailed ships. They floated on the smell of wax and remembered prayers. We stopped partway up the aisle, my breath catching in my throat. There, dangling in the corner, the companion ship to the one hanging in Fletcher's secret room— polished oak, cobalt keel, *The Champion*. I had the feeling we were underwater and these ships were wrecks drifting in the current. The air was honey, and I could almost reach Claire's outstretched hand. Then the world righted itself and the chapel carried us forward, we its only passengers.

Fletcher's ancestor's ship was beautifully wrought, the wood varnished, the sails gossamer. We stood under it and peered up. There was a figurehead on the prow that was missing from Fletcher's version. She looked like Dita, hair curling over bare shoulders, and her hand was extended as if flinging something into the sea. It pointed toward a clutch of metal hearts, high up on the wall of the apse.

I sensed the vial of liquid shuddering inside one of them. It only took a nudge to knock it from the wall. Walt grabbed at me when the metal clanged against the stone floor. The heart I'd plucked was tarnished silver, crowned and bulging. When I put my hand on it, the cold seared me. "*Ex-votos*," Walt said at my side, reading from the pamphlet. "Offerings from the wealthier sailors."

There was a hinge that creaked when we pried the case open. Inside, a small corked bottle of liquid and a piece of parchment, faded but legible, *Prayers for safe passage to King William Island, 1855.* It was signed "Drummond."

So it really was true. Drummond had been hired by Lady Jane to secretly search, to find proof that Franklin had died before any accounts of cannibalism, and if no proof existed, to construct it. Fletcher had said Drummond had added the postscript to the note that killed off Franklin, took him safely out of play. But why not just have Drummond return with his find and broadcast the news? Why leave it in the ice for another to discover, a risky plan at best?

Maybe Lady Jane had wanted an expert, someone with an impeccable reputation, to be the one to proclaim Franklin's innocence. And she found that person in McClintock, veteran of three previous expeditions, someone whose name the public would know and trust. So McClintock's *Fox* was purchased by Jane Franklin two years later, encouraged by her to find the cache, given directions attributed to a ghost girl or a psychic or to a woman's intuition honed by years of studying ships' logs. For the purposes of the historical record, the captain was dead and buried before his men grew desperate enough to feed on each other. His legacy was safe.

But this was barely proof. Even Fletcher's proud confession could simply have been family lore, embellished over the years. The letter from Jane Franklin that may have confirmed it was lost forever, reduced to the few fragments still tucked in my doctor's bag. It would have been a crazy plot, a spider's web of risk. I pocketed Drummond's prayer nonetheless, careful not to bend the delicate paper. In its place, in the chamber of the ex-voto, I left the dead woman's scrawl, her doodled valentines. The vial of melted snow I also left— in all likelihood, the last of the family's collection. I wished I had a piece of Claire to offer, but I didn't, so I used Walt's knife to pare the thinnest sliver of the callus built on my index finger by the stubborn old typewriter's keys. There was no blood, but the DNA that whorled that transparent flake sang my sister to me. So much we'd shared, and this would stay behind, small relic of our existence, charm against our vanishing.

MAMMALIAN DIVING REFLEX

*D*ARK LIKE NO OTHER. HE could not measure it. He could not find the stars to orient himself. His mind was not romantic enough to imagine them. Men kept falling through the ice and being hauled back up. At night they warmed the cask of rum by the fire until the spirits flowed honey-sluggish. The dram glass burned their lips. Everyone was blackened by the winter; no one was whole. He had lost things he could no longer remember, bits of flesh the least of them.

Night was the worst, and it was always night. Night was when men died. Sometimes they came back to life, gasping, bile spilling out of their throats, only to die again a little later. He, being the captain, said the last words for each of them. He marked their names in his book. The ink stank like lamp oil. He was tempted to drink it. Once, his stomach had been a live thing, then an empty leather bag, and now was a pebble that hardly swelled or shrank. In the dark, he plunged down, hoping. In the dark, he rose and made his count.

CHAPTER SIXTEEN

*W*E SET THE HEART AT the base of the wall, as if it had simply fallen. Some sexton would imagine minor earthquakes. As I turned to leave, Walt gently tugged me toward a small door on the side. He kept hold of my hand as we nudged it open and climbed a twisting, narrow set of stairs until we reached a landing beneath the steeple. He pointed up, and we leaned back against the railing, trusting the air between us and the street far below.

Looming above us was a stone woman, invisible from the front of the church, her arms outstretched, a constellation ringing her head. The sun was rising now, staining everything gold. "Star of the Sea," Walt said, and wheeled me around to see the harbor stretched before us, some of the boats looking as if they had been there a hundred years. We huddled into each other; the day was frigid, but clear. What a strange picture we must have made. The bear and the girl embracing. Except I was no girl in this fairy tale. If anything, I was the wolf, and he knew it. Why else had he fainted when first he saw me? Still, Walt held fast, and his warmth lulled me, as if it were I who had come into port and some beneficent spirit was raining fine-grained sparks of light upon me.

❄

Rembrandt had ripped a hole in the upholstery, dismantled the cup holder, and gnawed the plastic off the floor mat by the time we

218 • TINA MAY HALL

returned to the truck. Luckily, he was too lazy to attack the steering column or the gear shift. We wound our way back through the downtown of pale stone buildings, the sloping streets, the bundled-up youths trudging to early morning classes. My feet were glaciers despite the heat belching out of the pickup's vents. And my back was finally starting to twinge again, along with the scratches Dita had inflicted on my cheek. By midmorning, we were driving into Walt's town, and it was just as described: buildings whitewashed, signs hand-lettered, awnings bright, even in the snow.

❅

Walt's house was as shambling as he was, a rusty Victorian with tilting shutters, cupola perched like a miniature lighthouse at the peak. Next door to it, a renovated barn, all glass and concrete, galvanized accents, a witticism of modern repurposing. "My parents' house." Walt gestured at it. "They run the mail order side of things." Inside his cluttered kitchen, well-stocked with copper and crockery and assorted teapots, he drew a medic's kit in olive drab from beneath the sink and poked at my back cautiously. The blood had thickened the silk dress into a beetle's crust. He suggested a bath to loosen it, but I did not want to leave the kitchen, where I finally felt warm from tip to toe, my heart an oven stone. So Walt soaked towels in the sink and applied them to the great ache of my back, until the fabric began to pull free. Then he took up a gleaming filleting knife and pared the clothing from me, down to the leather of the boots. I was naked then, shining in his kitchen, and he stitched me so carefully, it didn't hurt a bit.

❅

For several weeks, the thaw had the land running with melted snow. The windows of Walt's house were liquid mirrors and the cupola a silver crown. In the mornings, roosters crowed and sheep bleated, the cows serenaded the college kids at milking time. Everything stretched to meet the sun. The reservoirs and rivers rose, and spring took hold. Lambs and calves were birthed by the dozens. Walt's parents came bearing jam and homemade liver snaps. They had the well-worn look of those who had trawled hell for a loved one and brought him up intact.

I wrote one last encyclopedia entry for my editor, but she wouldn't publish it, sent back words like *libel* and *fabrication*. So I returned to dowsing. Easy enough work in this part of the country, but everybody always wanted more water. They were exporting it now to many far-off places, and I always found the purest springs, the cold buried ones, the ones locked tight as a twin's heart.

Claire and I had never looked for love. We'd had each other. In the deep night, I still dreamt of her and woke drowning. Some nights, Walt was the one who woke up choking, his nostrils rimmed with sand. On those occasions, we trundled out of bed into the kitchen, where I'd help Walt punch the dough down and watch it rise back up. My loaves were always tough and withered. His floated, filled with sweet air.

✳

It took a few months before I was willing to go back to the village. When we returned at the last bloom of summer, we brought Drummond's prayer from the ex-voto and the fragments from Lady Jane's letter that had survived in my doctor's bag to add to the library's archive.

Harris was skinnier and more mustachioed than ever, afire with excitement over all the materials bequeathed to him from Fletcher's home. The story being bandied about town was that Eleanor had been embezzling from the gazebo fund and she and Fletcher had fled in disgrace to some warm locale. We had gone to see if my car was recoverable and found their house sleeping on the hill above town, boarded up, ringed in impenetrable black thorns. There was no sign of my car. Perhaps it was lost with the dead woman's, the ravine voracious as ever. No one in town mentioned Dita, but I suspected she'd found herself a sequined dress and joined Plover in his love affair with extinction. The map table was in the spot of honor in the main room of the library and never without a crowd of children playing with the mechanical men, staging races and dance productions, pouring glitter on the narwhal, taping up the seals' wounds.

The other items were all in the tower room, waiting to be catalogued. I slipped upstairs with my scraps of paper while Walt and Harris exchanged cookbook recommendations. The room was still dim; the sailors' voices still whispered. I tucked my rolled-up offerings into a porthole on the oak model of *The Champion*, which had been transplanted into a place of honor on the topmost shelf. One day, someone else would find them and make up a new story.

❄

In front of the coffee shop, the three fates still sat, now in undershirts, each holding a different-colored flyswatter. The heat had come down on us like a veil. Walt stopped to chat with them, and they each rubbed Rembrandt's smelly head in turn. I kept my distance, but they waved their swatters at me, a dubious benediction.

❄

I left Walt and Rembrandt happily munching pastries and conferring with the old men and drove up the hill past the site of my former house. It had been razed, insurance paid, land sold, planted by a local farmer, now knee-deep in flax plants, each studded with small flowers, a cloud of blue.

At Mariel's, I had to wait in the car until she could lead me to her door through the fog of bees. She parted them by ringing a golden bell, color of wings, clear as a waterfall. On the kitchen table stood a pot of tea next to a plate of cookies threaded with lavender. Mariel pulled a pen from her jar and two slips of paper. *Love* she wrote on one, *Lust* on the other, and pushed them across the table to me. I snatched them both up and crumpled them in my fist. My laugher and Mariel's saw screech rose together, and outside, the engineered bees paused midflight, heavy with all they had gathered, and shuddered in delight.

The sun spooled over the cottage. The turtle corpses in the garden burrowed more comfortably into the rich earth. In the faraway waters rising round us drifted ships laden with dead things, some terrible, some beautiful in their decay. No one knew if we would get another winter. Minute by minute, the world we rode was transformed, bone to coral, feather to web, ice to stone, and back again. Nine lemon pips had been plowed into the field downhill from us, and even now they were dreaming green.

ACKNOWLEDGMENTS

*J*HE RESOURCES ON VICTORIAN ARCTIC exploration I turned to again and again were the wonderfully detailed *Lady Franklin's Revenge* by Ken McGoogan, the beautifully illustrated exhibition catalog for *Ice: A Victorian Romance* mounted at the Linda Hall Library in 2008, and Sir John Franklin's account of his travels in the region prior to his fateful voyage, *Thirty Years in the Arctic Regions*.

Many thanks to the staff of the Scott Polar Research Institute at the University of Cambridge for allowing me to work with Lady Jane Franklin's letters and diaries, to the Corporation of Yaddo and Vermont Studio Center for providing residencies, to the National Endowment for the Arts for supporting writers, and to the Canadian Museum of History in Gatineau, Quebec, for staging a magnificent exhibit of the items brought up from Franklin's ships, which were found late in my writing process, but in time for a few details of those simultaneously eerie and mundane artifacts to make their way into the novel.

All the love to Michelle Dotter for her meticulous editing and keen eye and for reminding me to feed Rembrandt. A million thanks to Dzanc Books and Steve Gillis and Dan Wickett for their commitment to helping writers get their words into the world, and to Catherine Sinow for the day-to-day work of accomplishing this. And to Matt Revert for the absolutely gorgeous cover.

Thanks to my colleagues and students at Hamilton College for inspiring me daily; to Jenny Irons and George Hobor for letting me borrow lovely Lucy's habit of jumping out from behind trees so I could superimpose it on a creature with only a modicum of her beauty and grace; to Trudy Lewis for showing me how to make a writing life; and always, to Julio Videras for all of the wonderful walks where we remade the world through books.

Most of all, love to my parents, David and Kristy Hall, for their unwavering support and many unofficial writing retreats. And to Hoa, who knows where the bodies are buried. And to Tycho, best and brightest star in my sky.

❋

About the Author

Tina May Hall lives and teaches in upstate New York. Her collection of stories, *The Physics of Imaginary Objects*, won the 2010 Drue Heinz Literature Prize. She is the recipient of an NEA grant, and her stories have appeared in *SmokeLong Quarterly, The Collagist, Quarterly West, Black Warrior Review, Wigleaf,* and other journals.